Leaving Eldorado

Leaving Eldorado

JOANN MAZZIO

HOUGHTON MIFFLIN COMPANY
Boston   1993

Copyright © 1993 Joann Mazzio

All rights reserved. For information about permission
to reproduce selections from this book, write to
Permissions, Houghton Mifflin Company, 215 Park Avenue
South, New York, New York 10003.

Library of Congress Cataloging-in-Publication Data

Mazzio, Joann.
  Leaving Eldorado / Joann Mazzio.
    p.   cm.
  Summary: In the late 1890s, after her gold-mad father abandons her
in the small New Mexico Territory mining town of Eldorado, fourteen-
year-old Maude struggles to survive and to hold onto her dream of
becoming an artist.
  ISBN 0-395-64381-3
  [1. Frontier and pioneer life — New Mexico — Fiction.   2. New
Mexico — Fiction.   3. Artists — Fiction.]   I. Title.
PZ7.M47815Le   1993   92-13853
[Fic] — dc20   CIP
                             AC
Printed in the United States of America
AGM 10 9 8 7 6 5 4 3 2 1

For Lee and Jim — my all the world

PROLOGUE

Mama, it's been over a month now since you left me. Da and Uncle Rab spend the week up at their claim, only coming in on a Saturday to get supplies.

I pass my days and nights alone except for Daisy. Of course, I don't spend my nights with Daisy. She's tethered under the lean-to.

In my mind I talk with you, but your voice is getting faint. I'm going to try writing my thoughts on this tablet to hold your attention. You were always a great one for reading.

I do need your attention and help, Mama. Being of the age of fourteen like I am puts me close to being a grown woman. But, as you know, I'm inexperienced in the ways of the world and my powers of judgment are not developed.

Dear Mama, you are probably anxious to join the angels in Heaven, but please stay by my side for just a little while longer.

It won't be for long, Mama, only until I can stand on my own feet. I don't plan on writing my life story in this tablet. My life story is what I'm going to live just as soon as I feel competent to undertake it.

Sunday, December 20, 1896

Mama, I'm writing now because I'm disturbed by what happened last night.

The day was dark and lowering and night came on fast. After eating some beans and a biscuit, I tried drawing out some pictures on the back of a smooth shingle. You remember we ran out of coal oil while you were still here, Mama, and I've not had any for the lamp since. So I built up the fire with the punky cottonwood, which was all the wood I had. If our dugout had windows, it would have made no difference yesterday, the gloom was so deep.

The firelight wasn't bright enough for drawing, so I gave it up and went to bed. Lying there brought back to me the many nights we spent there together. Sometimes you went feverish and sweaty from your illness. Other times you talked about your girlhood home in the green hills of Virginia and how you were going to take me there to visit after you got better and Da struck the rich vein of gold he was always searching for.

When the wood flared up in the stove, light played on the muslin ceiling I've got overhead. Even if I did make it myself, that ceiling gives me a great satisfaction.

2

In the middle where the muslin sags down almost to head level, there's a big smiling sun-face with curly rays. Angels surround the sun, with feathers molting from their fancy wings. In the corners there are fish and rabbits and birds. Over the bed, Mama, I made a likeness of you. You're all golden and pretty, sitting with a little girl on your lap. The little girl might be me when I was little. I ran out of crayons before I finished, so the girl is not complete. She looks like she's trying to push away from the mother and slide to the floor.

When you were so sick, Mama, before the end, dust would fall from the soddy roof. It would fall onto your pale, fevered face and make a mustache around your mouth. I said to Father, "Da, it's not right Mama should look so foolish when she's so sick." He gave me money then for muslin. But, Mama, you died before I could get it fixed up.

I was so sad and mournful that I cried on the muslin and spotted it. I was a pitiful sight. You would have told me to blow my nose and buck up. But working on the muslin did the same thing for me. I ironed the muslin with the sadiron to set the color. Then I sewed the strips together. When Da was home for the weekend, he helped me to hang it all across the ceiling. The dust and bugs can't fall through anymore. Da seemed surprised by all the work, but he didn't say it was any good or pretty. It's probably just ugly daubing. But making it did make me feel better.

Last night I had almost drifted into sleep when I heard a noise outside our house. In an instant, I clutched the poker I keep beside the bed just like you told me. Soon

3

I heard Da's voice, booming big, and Uncle Rab's voice skittering along, too, like a buzzing fly trying to keep up with a horse. From what they said, I knew they came in earlier in the day from their dig and went straight to the Mercantile Bar. Oh, Mama, I know he works hard, but I do think Da spends too much time and money in that bar. Maybe that's because he misses you and that's his way of grieving, but still I don't think it's good.

After Da and Uncle Rab put Lefty in the stall, they came in, still talking and laughing loud until Da saw me. I pretended to be asleep because Da's sometimes hard on me when he's been drinking. He said, "Shh" and giggled like a little boy.

They drew the curtain across the room and hung their lighted lantern on a peg. From the noises I knew they were getting biscuits out of the larder and dipping into the pot of beans I left on the back of the stove. Soon they were at the table and talking low.

Most of what I could hear, I heard before. Their claim is worked out, and they've got no money to buy a new one. An honest man can't make a living. All the placer deposits are worked out, and it takes big companies to work the lodes. Big companies with big money. Da's big voice would state the matter, and Uncle Rab's voice would run along saying, "Yep. That's so. Yep, you got that right."

When Da ran down, Uncle Rab said, "Maybe we better hire on with Continental or Solomon's company, just for the winter."

"Never. I'm blamed if I'll be a company man."

"Shucks, Johnnie, I'm with you one hundred percent.

But we need some money, and we're not getting doodly squat from our mine. You know what the Mexicans say. The poor find the mines, the simple work them, and the rich profit by them."

"That's the God's truth."

"Maybe we could sign on with the Tic-Tac-Toe Ranch for a spell. I've done some cowboying in my day. I hear that if Collins can get his herd rounded up, he's got a contract to deliver around a thousand head to the military this spring."

"Now, Rab, I ain't no cowboy. I'm a prospector and miner, and my turn is coming. I'm always getting to these gold and silver strikes too late, after all the best claims are taken. I tell you what, Rab, we gotta get to that Klondike strike and get in on the ground floor."

"Yeah, Yukon Territory. That's the place. Nuggets big as pigeon eggs, they say. Just pick them up off the ground."

What with the drone of talking I was dozing, but I woke up plenty fast when I heard that. Even under the warm covers, Mama, I shivered. The way those names sounded — Yukon, Klondike — it was just like matches striking. Like matches lighting a blaze.

Though I was very young when we left Colorado to come here, I remember Da's voice, sort of Jubilee-sounding, saying, "Eldorado, New Mexico Territory. They're picking gold nuggets off the ground there. As big as eggs."

His voice is Jubilee-sounding again. I'm fearful he's got the gold fever and is not likely to get rid of it.

I heard Uncle Rab say in a wise voice, the one he uses with me when he's pretending to be my real uncle, "I hear it's a mite cold up there, Johnnie. Lots of snow. Short summers."

"Cold," Da said, snorting. "I followed that gold bug from Wyoming to Deadwood, from Leadville to Silver Reef. It's cold in them Rockies, and the snow don't hardly ever let up. But it's my turn, I tell you, Rab. There's signs if you know where to look for them. Like omens. And I know the Yukon is where I'm going to make my big strike. I am going to be a millionaire in this new century coming up. My left hand has been itching ever since I heard the word Yukon. That's a sign you're going to get wealth, you know."

"You're sure about that? I always thought it meant you're going to meet a stranger."

"Leave the signs to me, Rab. You're thinking about the right hand. If that itches, it means you're going to shake hands with a stranger."

"I thought that meant you were going to kiss a pretty girl."

"Rab," Da pure roared at Uncle Rab, "an itchy nose means you're going to kiss a pretty girl. Now just never mind all that. I've seen the signs, and they tell me to go to the Yukon."

Silence fell between them. The pounding of the stamping mill over on the other side of town thudded on regular as a heartbeat. You know how it is, Mama. That pounding goes on day and night, and you don't notice it except at special times when it seems to grow loud and fill up every space.

6

"It would take quite a grubstake, Johnnie. More blankets and heavy clothing than we got here," Uncle Rab said.

"Yeah. Two train tickets from here to San Francisco and two steamer passages from San Francisco to Alaska," my father said.

Three. I thought, "Don't you mean three, Da?" I waited to hear Da's voice correct himself.

But it was Uncle Rab who said, "You mean three, Johnnie. There's little Maude to be considered."

"To be sure. To be sure, Rab."

"It's going to be rough up there, Johnnie. No place for a woman."

"Yeah, I know. And Maude's not full-grown yet. She's only . . . I don't recollect how old she is."

Mama, I was that surprised that my own father couldn't remember my age. Fourteen, I wanted to yell. But I stayed quiet, even if it was deceitful. The time was past when I should have spoken out. Besides, I was confused. Maybe Da didn't really want to take me along.

"Well, whatever her age," Da continued, "I can't just go off and leave her."

"I reckon not," Uncle Rab said. He continued, "Didn't you mail a letter to your wife's folks back East?"

"Yeah. Sylvia had me mail a letter. She asked her brother to take Maude and educate her if Sylvia should pass on. Then when Sylvia did go, Maude asked me to mail another letter."

"What do you think about that idea, Johnnie?"

"Not much, Rab. This brother, he's supposed to be a

lawyer. Sylvia and me, we were married, oh, twenty, twenty-one years. She used to write to him. We never heard back all that time, and there were times when it would have done her a world of good to hear from her family."

My father choked up some and had to stop and blow his nose. He misses you, too, Mama.

But he's wrong about Uncle Oscar, isn't he, Mama? Right after you passed away, when I wrote to tell him, I said just as plain as I knew how that I would need traveling money to come to him. I promised I would pay him back. I know that's what you would want me to say because we have pride in our family and don't take charity from anyone. Not even kin.

His letter should come any day now. Then I can travel to Virginia, where I can see dogwood trees and smell magnolia blossoms and pick trilliums in the deep woods. I can go to a proper school and learn the proper way to do things. Mama, I'm just thirsting to see the beautiful homes and the green mountains of Virginia.

It's not your fault, Mama, but my whole memory is of living in mining camps. Thrown-together houses far from water and firewood. All the trees cut down and the streets and alleys so muddy or dusty you can't keep anything clean. And this place, Eldorado, it's been the worst. It was no wonder you couldn't get well, living in this soddy. I can't even call it a house. It's more like a den, fit for animals. Dug into the canyon-side, covered with a sod roof. When the snow starts to melt, the water seeps in and everything gets muddy. The woodcutters' burros going up the canyon kick rocks and dirt off the trail above our roof so that I fear they're going to start a slide and bury us someday.

Mama, after thinking about Da's slip of the tongue concerning the tickets, my confusion cleared up. I know now that I don't want to live in the Klondike or Eldorado or any other mining camp. Mama, please help the letter to come so I can leave here and go to Virginia.

Sunday, December 27, 1896

Mama, I have come to the cemetery for two reasons. No, three reasons. I wanted to be near your grave so I can write to you better. It's quieter here, with the fence all around to keep the hogs and dogs out. You can still hear the stamping mill, but there's no place you can get away from that. The soot sifts down, too.

It's the only place in town that's got a bit of grass. I scraped the snow off and have Daisy tethered so she can get some browse. So, Daisy is my second reason. Da went back to his dig this week and didn't leave me any money to buy hay. Daisy's awful thin, and I'm just getting a little milk each evening from her. I asked myself what you would do. I almost heard your voice, strong, like it was before you took sick, saying, "Buy hay." So, I did and told the feed store to put it on Da's bill. But I'm doling it out to Daisy so it will last.

My last reason is it's almost pretty here. I wish you could see how the snow has mounded up on the older graves. They have the look of crouching animals, hibernating. Waiting for spring to come so they can stand up and throw off the snow and plod away over the mountains. You'd laugh at the sight.

The snow has melted off your grave, Mama. It's so

raw-looking it makes me hurt. But I've made something for you. Your own hibernating creature. I gathered snow from under the junipers where the smoke hasn't dirtied it. Now you have an alabaster rabbit crouched right against your wood marker. I patted snow and shaped it with my hands. The ears go straight back on the head, and you can even see the nose and eyes.

You know, Mama, I don't have any idea what you can see. I feel you're right with me. Right inside me, sometimes, especially when I write in this tablet. But, in case you can't see, I'll tell you.

Uncle Rab got a nice piece of plank and he smoothed it some and rounded the top. He's a pretty good carver, and he took great pains with this. GONE TO BE WITH THE ANGELS, it says. Sylvia Swinbun Brannigan. April 20, 1857–November 11, 1896.

It makes me think of those other headboards, the little ones for the babies that were born before me. In cemeteries in Utah and Colorado. Leslie, Ariel, Mariette, Rose, Peale. Gone to be with the angels, too. Even their names are light and airy. Not substantial like mine. It's no wonder they didn't find a foothold in the rocky soil of mining camps.

I'm glad you gave me a good solid name, Mama. Maude Oakley Brannigan. It's strong like I am. When I was in school right here in Eldorado, it was a burden at times. Those foolish boys would call me "Mud." Then when they learned my middle name, they plagued me further by yelling, "Timber." But I caught one of them and rubbed mud in his mouth, and that put an end to that.

Your name is fairylike, too, Mama. As light as you

were in your last days. I could lift you and bathe you.

Do you know that I laid you out, Mama? I just went ahead and did it myself before I told anyone about you. I'd been taking care of you most of the last year. It was just natural that I would bathe you and dress you in your best dress. Then I went for the preacher at the Methodist Church, and he said I did a good job. Did you know that I did that, Mama? Or were you too excited by passing over into the Glory Land to pay attention to what was happening here?

When it came time for the funeral, I didn't have anything fit to wear. I went in your trunk and got one of your dresses. The hem struck me well up on the calf, but I had to wear it anyway. So, there you were in the grave in your best, and there I was in your second-best looking down at you.

I've got another reason to be writing, Mama. I should get on with it instead of blithering around like this. This headstone I'm sitting on is feeling colder all the time. You probably know how troubled I am. As I told you, last Saturday night I heard Da and Uncle Rab talking about going off to the Yukon to the new gold strike. But Da never said a word to me the next day. Just mended some of the burro's gear. He had me running hither and yon, fetching this and that. When I stopped to break off an icicle that looked like the crystal horn of a fairy-tale unicorn, he yelled at me. Without letting up, he kept at me all day. Cook this, bake that. When I tried to tell him there wasn't enough wood, he called me lazy and no-good. I know he's not mean-turned, Mama. Since you left, though, I can't seem to do anything to please him. To keep from being a burden to him, I try to do everything he wants.

I wonder that he didn't mention anything about leaving Eldorado. But nary a word. Just packed Lefty the burro and went back to the mine with Uncle Rab. Maybe it was just the whiskey talking last Saturday night.

I was alone all this week until he came in on Saturday. Friday was Christmas. I made a pine wreath for the door, but since we've only got the canvas flap covering the entrance, I just staked that wreath onto the sod roof. It was kind of sad-looking. I lighted a candle for my supper table.

But there was nothing to be sad about except missing you, Mama. I have food on my table and a roof over my head. When Da came in on Saturday, he had a present for me. It was nothing I had ever wished for. Nevertheless, I showed him my true gratitude for thinking of me. What he gave me was a grown-up lady's hat. It's the kind that looks like a plate with lots of net and stuff on it. Black, it is. Kind of pretty. Like a dead bird. I don't know what possessed him to buy me a hat like that. It's for a grown-up lady. Even if I was a grown-up lady, I can't see me wearing the hat to fetch firewood or milk Daisy. What I need is boots. But what I wanted was wax crayons. They had a box at the Mercantile before Christmas. I reckon they're gone now. Someone with money, from the mining companies, maybe, bought them for his children.

I wonder. Does Da think that hat will be the thing to wear in the Yukon? It must be cold up there. I don't want to go to one more mining camp.

13

Gold fever. It's a sickness. Da's never going to get over it. He's going to spend his life running from one place to another on this planet. Those places are going to be like Eldorado. Some worse, I guess, than where we live now.

Mama, if Da does pick up and leave here, I need your help. I'm going to stay and wait for the letter from Uncle Oscar. But Da's got a golden tongue for talking people into doing what he wants. You've always said that. Please help me have the strength to resist. And, if you can, help the letter get here soon.

School's in session again. While I'm waiting for the letter, I'd like to go to school, but my clothes aren't fit. I'd be shamed to go in these layers of rags I wear, with my feet poking out the toe of my boots. There's so much I need to learn, it'd almost be worth putting up with the shame. I do try to shape my letters careful as I write this so I don't forget my penmanship.

I remember when I first started school in Eldorado. You had your health, and we rented a real house. When I went to school, I was as curled and starched as Miss Katy herself. When some of the others stood by the stove in the middle of the room, they stank like pee. They had to sleep in the same bed with little ones, and, of course, they slept in the same shifts they wore under their clothes. Miss Katy and some of us others would move away from the stove, even if it was colder, and sort of look at each other. No one said anything.

The butter money I saved went to pay, well, expenses. And Daisy's going dry. She doesn't give enough milk for churning. My clothes are outgrown and worn-out.

14

It's sometimes hard to get enough water heated for bathing, let alone washing clothes. All the perfumes in Araby probably wouldn't cover up the stench I'd make if I stood by a hot stove now. I wouldn't want to be in a schoolroom where others moved away from me.

*

Mama, the strangest thing happened just now. I was just sitting, huddled up and quiet, trying to push the noise of the stamping mill out of my mind so I could hear you if you took a notion to visit with me.

A bluejay, a gust of wind, or something shook the branches of the juniper next to me. Snow exploded into the air and the sun made the crystals sparkle like a cloud of glory.

The strangeness, Mama, of seeing so much beauty shower down over such ugliness. Oh, that radiance. Maybe I should take it for a sign that things are going to work out all right. But I can't believe in that kind of superstition.

Did you have anything to do with it, Mama? Are you trying to teach me something that I'm too ignorant to understand?

Saturday, January 2, 1897

Oh, Mama, I need your strength to sustain me now. As the Bible puts it — I am sore afraid. My New Year is starting off by looking very black.

Da and Uncle Rab came in from their diggings on Thursday and brought all their gear with them. Instead of going to the Mercantile Bar, they came straight here. Da was stone-cold sober.

It was a bright day, and I was sitting on a rock beside the trail in the sun. I had found a dry tree root that seemed to have a likeness in it. I had whittled it with my knife until I was just beginning to see Chinese features like Yee's — you might remember the Chinese cook from the Palmer House? I never heard Da until he was right on top of me. I started like a deer.

He sat down beside me and took my carving out of my hand. "I'll be doggone. If that don't take all. That's the spitting image of Yee at the Palmer House."

Then he set the carving down and looked at me direct. "Maude," he said, "we're fixing to pull out of here. Me and Rab and you. We're going to the Klondike." Even though I had been waiting for this very conversation, the word "Klondike" still sent a shiver up my spine like fingernails on slate. I drew in my breath and sat quiet, trying to keep my hands still in my lap.

"You know I'm not making enough out of that claim to live on. All the placer claims around here are worked out. There's just the two deep mines, and I will not work in them."

"But in the Yukon, now," he continued, "if we can get there fast, we'll be in at the beginning. It's those that get to a gold strike first who make out best. It's my turn to hit the big pay dirt. I've just been getting to the strikes as they're petering out. But this time is it, Maude. I'm doing this for the both of us. I'm not waiting to dig at some other man's leavings. I'll get there first. You'll see. The signs are right." His voice lapped and crackled like butter in a hot skillet. Mama, you know. You always said his gold was in his tongue.

"Da," I tried to say.

But he rushed on. "Go to school. A proper school. Back East. And clothes. When I strike it rich, you'll have anything you want. Furs, even. Diamonds. We'll build a house. Big house in San Francisco. That's where lots of fellows build houses when they strike it rich. You'll like San Francisco. You can have servants. A carriage, even, with your own horses. Think of that."

He finally remembered why he was talking to me and stopped. He studied my face.

I said, "Da, I don't want to."

He slapped his hand on his knee. "You mean don't want to have servants and horses? Well, that'd be all right. No need to buy what you don't want. You'd probably like to have oil paintings and statues, wouldn't you?

17

That'd be fine. You could always borrow my carriage. Or Rab's."

"No, Da. I mean I don't want to go to the Yukon at all."

"You'd rather stay in this run-down place and starve?"

"Da, remember the letter you mailed for me? After Mama passed away? Well, I know there'll be an answer soon. I just know there will. Then I'll go live with Uncle Oscar and his family in Virginia."

"Maude, Maude. You can't count on hearing from your Ma's folks. That's just a pipe dream." He continued, "I can't leave you here alone waiting for a letter that likely won't come."

"I'd be all right, Da. I stay by myself all through the week anyway. No one thinks to harm me."

"They dasn't touch you while you're under my protection. They know they'd have me to deal with if they so much as harmed a hair on your head." He added, "And so much the worse now that you're turning into a woman."

Seeing Da acknowledge that I was growing up, I tried something else. "Da, I could probably get a job while I wait for the letter. Maybe up at the Palmer House. Lovey was my friend at school. Maybe she'd speak to her mother about putting me on there."

Da rared up and started roaring. "A daughter of mine working in a boardinghouse? Around those dirty-minded miners? What would your poor mother think?"

"Da, you know it's a respectable place. Mrs. Steckler is so respectable she looks like it hurts."

"No. No. No," he roared, shaking his head from side to side till his black beard quivered.

"Da, I'm not going to live in mining camps all my life. When I get the letter, I'm leaving here. Even if I have to earn my own travel money."

"Earn enough to travel," Da said, sneering. "All by yourself? What do you expect to do? Sell your body?"

It took my breath away that Da should talk to me so rude. He knows I could never become a bad woman.

Mama, I'm ashamed to say, I lost my temper and said something bold, something I'd never said aloud to anyone, not even you. I said, "I'm leaving here. I'm planning on making something of myself. I'm going to be an artist when I grow up. I'm going to paint beautiful pictures like Michael Angelo did."

"What can you be thinking, girl? You can't be an artist. Women aren't artists. There's never been a woman artist."

I wish I hadn't said it. It is a dream that I had never put into words before because I, too, have so many doubts about it. There probably aren't any women artists. It's probably not allowed, just as women aren't allowed to do so many other things.

My temper cooled down. I held my head down while I fussed at my boots, sticking the packing back into the toe.

Finally, Da ran out of scorn to heap on my head. I ventured to say, "Wouldn't it be easier to pay for two passages instead of three, Da? I don't want to be a burden on you."

"Don't you worry about that. You're supposed to be

19

a burden until you're grown. But you are right. Money is in short supply. We're figuring to sell the cow and the burro and all our gear to get train tickets to San Francisco. Then we're fixing to work a little to get money for our passage to Alaska. You could help maybe. A place like San Francisco, you could maybe get work at a boardinghouse."

As worked up as I was, I had to smile. Now that working in a boardinghouse was part of his plan, it was all right. He saw me smiling. I said, "What would my poor mother think?"

Being caught out in his argument like that seemed to turn him in his thinking.

"Well, maybe if we left you the cow . . . Just maybe, I'm saying. I was just your age when I left home." I wondered if he had finally figured out how old I was, but I didn't interrupt him. He went on, "I made out all right. Of course, I was a boy. But then you're better educated. You write a better hand than I do right now. Also, the way you nursed your mother. You learned lots there. You might make your way being a nurse or something if you was to leave here. Then, there's the letter. Stranger things have happened. It could come."

I held my breath, letting Da work his argument on himself.

He looked at me sharply. "I guess the Palmer House ain't too bad. You're smart enough to take care of yourself if things do get rough. You think there's a good chance you can get on there?"

"Yes, Da. I've got to ask, but I suspect there's a good chance. Mrs. Steckler would look after me until the letter comes."

He slapped his hands on his thighs and stood up. "It's settled then. You stay. As for me, I'm going for the whole hog," he said. Although Da was committing himself to a life of danger and hard work, he seemed as pleased as Punch.

"Come inside. There's something I must do."

He had me sit at the table with paper and pen. I wrote what he told me, in his exact words. He made over his claim and this soddy to me. After he signed, he yelled to Uncle Rab to come in and witness.

"Are you leaving Daisy to me, Da? I'll need a bill of sale if I ever sell her."

I noticed Da didn't meet Uncle Rab's eyes. Uncle Rab looked a little anxious. Then he started smiling and said, "You're a real lady of property, now, ain't you? If I'd had a start like this when I was your age, I'd be a millionaire by this time, most probably."

Da found the creased bill of sale in his leather wallet. He signed it over to me.

I was excited and happy and fearful and sad all at the same time. To keep from thinking about my feelings, I got busy baking up biscuits and frying out fatback for Da and Uncle Rab to pack for their train trip. I mended his extra shirt and underwear and hunted up tools that had been mislaid.

Sunday, January 3, 1897

They left early this morning walking down the mountain to Santa Cecilia to catch the train. They're going to sell Lefty and their tools and gear to buy their train tickets. I hope they have enough to cover them. I walked out with them as far as the Divide. Da hugged me tight, and I felt like a little girl. We were both crying. Though he's so happy to be striking out for the Yukon, I know he feels bad about leaving me behind.

I came back to the dugout, and it looks like a strange place even though I've got the papers to it. I'm sitting at the table here wrapped in your quilt, the linsey-wool-sey one you brought as part of your hope chest all the way from Virginia. The sun is shining bright outside, but I feel chilled.

Maybe I made a big mistake by not going with Da. I don't feel grown-up enough to be all alone. I feel like a poor motherless child.

Mama, I pray you to be with me and comfort me.

Monday, January 18, 1897

I can scarce stand this waiting, Mama. The mail comes by stage from Santa Cecilia and gets here about noon. I'm waiting now to hear the noon whistle from the Continental Mine.

Trying to keep busy this morning so I wouldn't think too much about being alone, I carried water from the spring and put it in a tub in the sunshine to heat. Then I took Daisy up along the trail so she could get some fresh grass. But the woodcutters' burros have eaten every blade of grass, including the roots. We climbed the mountain until we came onto pretty deep snow. I found an old canvas pannier someone had thrown away.

I drove Daisy back home and let her eat some of the precious hay. The canvas came in handy as a patch over a corner of the roof that was leaking.

It's muddy all up and down the trail. Water seeps into the house and turns this dirt floor to mud. I look down at my boots sometimes, and they're so muddy I look like I'm taking root in the ground. A real Mud Oak-ley.

The water warmed up some, so I washed my other set of underclothes. I'm always bashful about hanging them out on the fence. Though no one lives around here, there's always someone going up and down the trail.

I feel pretty safe at night. I went down to Mr. Reese's house and borrowed the iron head frame from his bed. At night, I wire that across the entrance from the inside. I sleep light, too. So far, no one interferes with my solitary way of life.

So while I'm waiting for the noon whistle, I'm writing this to pass the time. I'll tell you what my walk to the Post Office is like — just as when you were sick in bed, I described everything to you that I did outside the house.

I go down the trail and cross Elk Creek by the foot log. The water is high because of the snow melting higher up in the mountains. The Frying Pan Claim is just an empty hole in the ground with no one working it. There's still some broken tools and a cradle sitting there. You remember how we used to see Mr. Reese shoveling gravel in that very cradle and his partner rocking it and running water through it. It makes me think of Da and Uncle Rab's claim. I've not been up there in recent days, but I expect it looks pretty much like this one.

Mr. Reese's house is empty. Someone said he went to California. The door is gone. When I got the head frame, I saw that rats have nested in the straw pallet on the bed.

Da is right. This town has seen its best days.

The trail comes out on Church Street, and there the mud is deeply rutted from the wagons. The hogs are as big a nuisance as they ever were. People are still laughing about them and saying they're our garbage department. It does seem like folks could keep the pigs in a pen and bring the garbage to them. Instead, people just throw their slops out the door into the yard or street and let the hogs wander around eating whatever they can find.

And the dogs. They're everywhere, yipping and howling and seeming to belong to no one. At least the hogs are useful for food. If we were more like the Indians we could make a tasty stew out of these hounds.

School's in session. The door stands open during the day to take advantage of the sunshine. When you pass you can hear the students reciting. Not ten feet away, I have to get off the boardwalk because there are always three or four boys sprawled there, none more than ten years old. They play cards, smoke, and pitch pennies at a crack in the boardwalk. They curse like men. The air is blue from the way they talk.

There's Mrs. Anderson's nice yard with the white picket fence. The white scrolls on her porch roof are pretty. She planted poplars last summer, and they're going to look real nice when spring comes. The building where there used to be a barbershop is empty. The bank building is empty, too. I heard Da say they aren't going to reopen it. People are leaving Eldorado.

When we first came here, you remember there were big plans for the town. Paving the streets, piping water to each house. There's no sign of that now. Eldorado looks like it's heading the way of other camps that have turned into ghost towns. For now, the two big deep mines are working only two shifts. But the stamping mill goes day and night. Pounding, pounding.

The Methodist Church was just finished this year.

25

You never got to see it. It looks nice, too, with its adobe walls and wood-shingled roof. The sign by the door says it was built by the generous donation of Mrs. Hastings. She is the wife of Continental's president, and they say she does good works in all the mining camps where they have mills and mines. I guess Da was thinking about people like the Hastings family when he said we'd be millionaires and live in San Francisco. For that's where they live. Where the streets are paved.

The Methodist preacher lives just across the street, and it was him I fetched after I laid you out.

Then it's on past the Poor House and the Pest House. Both miserable places. For me, the Poor House has little to recommend it over the Pest House. In the Pest House one could die of disease of the body, but in the Poor House one could die of disease of the spirit.

After these buildings, I turn and go down past the Fire House. This is always a tribulation because of the volunteers hanging around the front. Sometimes they have the water wagon pulled out, working on it. Most of the time they aren't doing anything but just sitting out front whittling and gawking. I walk by with my head up, looking neither to the right or left. I can't help but hear what they're saying. But I let on that I can't.

Once I knew they were talking about me and wanting me to hear. One said, "Gather ye rosebuds while ye may." Another said, "Forget that rosebud. That one's a rosebud I'm going to pick for myself." Then they both gave those big jackass laughs like young men do. Imagine them thinking they know anything about poetry.

How is it if you're a girl, you can be going by, not

giving any mind to the foolishness of such as them, and they can say something or look a certain way as to make you feel all dirty and ashamed? Mama, is just being a girl about to be a woman something to be ashamed of?

*

Mama, Mama, what am I to do now? I just went to the Post Office. The letter was finally there. It was addressed to Da, but I claimed it. I stuck it in my pocket and fairly flew home where I could read it in private.

Being where you are, you probably know already about your brother, Oscar. He's dead. The letter was written by somebody at a bank. He said Uncle Oscar never married. Remember how we used to picture him enjoying life at your old family house with his loving family around him? There wasn't any family. There wasn't even any old family home for the last ten years. The letter said the estate was "disbursed" to pay off bills arising from Uncle Oscar's "debilitating and lingering" illness. Sincerest condolences, it said.

My heart sinks. With you gone and my father somewhere on his way to the Yukon, I am truly alone. Oh, now I wish I had gone straightaway to ask Mrs. Steckler for a job like I told Da I would.

Mama, I know you're trying to help me. I can almost hear your voice saying, "You'll be all right, my Maude. You've got true grit." I hope I can live up to your faith in me.

Tuesday afternoon, January 19, 1897

Mama, I'm trying to put the letter behind me. Going back East to live with Uncle Oscar is a peg I can no longer hang my hopes on. My disappointment is bitter, but I cannot sink into despair.

I must find a job and a place to live. My flour and lard have run out. The beans and potatoes are almost gone. Last night, with not enough wood to keep a fire going, I half froze. Then I was wakened by shouting and the sound of metal clanging. I was scared out of my wits. Thinking it was a hanging or drunk cowboys tearing up the camp, I crouched in the dark behind my barricaded door like a rabbit run to ground in a miserable burrow. I must use that true grit you say I have to make my own way in this world.

Yesterday at the Post Office, I overheard two women talking. They said Lovey and her new husband, a Mr. Washburn, had just returned from their honeymoon. It was the first I heard of Lovey being married. She's just the same age as I am. It's hard for me to imagine that fate for myself.

I determined this very day to renew my friendship with Lovey. First, I need friends. A person cannot talk to her departed mother and a cow forever. Second, I wanted to ask if she'll help me get a job at the Palmer House.

Mama, you would probably like to hear about my visit to see Lovey.

When she used to come after school to play with me, when we still lived in the rented house, you would smile a little smile at some of the things Lovey said. I didn't know why your smile was so unsmiling. I haven't seen her much these last two years, what with her going to school and working at the Palmer House and me staying home with you.

I cleaned up and dressed the best I could. My underclothes were still damp, but, not having any others, I put them on anyway. I wrapped my new hat in a pillowcase and put it in my shopping basket.

The newlyweds live in the third frame house past the Methodist Church. It's not painted, but it does have a corrugated roof and wood-plank floors. A bit of smoke came from the stovepipe. The lace curtains and the window blinds looked new. As I knocked on the door, I kept clearing my throat, I was that nervous. I didn't know what to expect.

Lovey opened the door. She looked uncertain at first, then said, "Maude. Come in." Over a cotton dress that came to her ankles, she wore an apron. Her hair was piled up on her head and kind of frizzy in front. Not so long ago, we were jumping rope together. Now, here she was, acting dignified and old. She smiled from a great distance as though she might ask me, "How old are you, little girl?"

"May I show you my house?" she asked. She kept her left hand moving around in the air between us until I caught on and asked to see her rings.

"Well, just a wedding ring now. Mr. Washburn says he'll buy me an engagement ring later. We weren't engaged, you know. Just up and left. Got married down in Santa Cecilia, then went to El Paso for our honeymoon."

"Oh, Maude," she squealed, sounding for the first time like she used to when we were friends, "you ought to see El Paso."

"I purely want to," I replied. As you remember, Mama, you and I never set foot off this mountainside once we moved here. I've never since been back to Santa Cecilia, just eight miles down the road from here.

"We stayed in a hotel. The Marlboro Hotel. It was grand. Three stories. Right down the hall from our room there was a bathroom with running water. Water that you don't have to carry bucket by bucket to take a bath. Can you imagine that?" She ran on. "There were people, nice-dressed people everywhere. And wagons, and buggies, and horses. Shops, all kinds of shops."

"Was it pretty?" I asked.

"Not pretty, exactly. The streets were too dusty. But it was exciting. It's much warmer there. Mr. Washburn says it's because El Paso is further south and much lower in altitude than Eldorado."

"You call your husband Mr. Washburn?" I asked.

"Well, yes. It seems proper, him being twenty-four years old and all. I think married people should respect each other, don't you?"

Lovey didn't wait for answers. All the while she showed me the bought chairs, stuffed with horsehair, the bed and dresser and the kitchen, she talked.

"I bought material for the curtains and lots of other stuff in El Paso. 'Just get what you're going to need,' Mr. Washburn said. Prices aren't so dear there as they are here. Isn't this pattern on the oilcloth pretty?"

Before I could answer, she said, "Oh, I almost forgot my manners. I'm not used to being a married woman yet. May I offer you some coffee? There's some still hot on the stove. We can sit here."

I was in sort of a daze because Lovey jumped back and forth from being the old Lovey to being the new married woman. But I agreed quite freely that everything looked nice. The oilcloth on the table, the lace curtains, the yellow monk's cloth curtains between the front room and the kitchen. Lovey looked and sounded quite happy, and somehow triumphant, like she did when she won the Friday spelling bee at school.

I finally remembered my manners and wished her the best in her marriage and gave her the hat. She jumped up from the table and ran to the bedroom to try it on. She knew how to stick a hatpin through it to hold it to the top of her hair. Turning this way and that to look at herself in the mirror over the dresser, she did look older. Only the strands of dark blond hair that escaped from her hairpins and waved about her thin neck made her look like a little girl playing dress-up.

Standing in back of her, I almost didn't know my own reflection. Being taller, I can easily see over the top of Lovey's head. My hair's darker red than I remember it being and also long and bushy. My eyebrows and eye-lashes have darkened, too, so they look more like Da's. I guess I'm going to be tall like he is. I don't believe I've got my full growth yet. It's been a while since I've seen my own reflection in anything but the water pail or an occasional window.

Lovey caught me looking at myself. "You ought to doll up a little, Maude. You're never going to catch a beau until you fix up a little."

"That's not my aim right now, Lovey," I said. I explained about Da leaving and how I needed a job.

"I'm not going to stay in Eldorado, Lovey," I said. "I have to make enough money to get out of here before this place kills me like it did Mama."

Lovey looked upset. "You mean you have consumption, too? That was what she died of, wasn't it?"

"No, I'm healthy as a horse. All this ugliness — that's what I can't stand."

"Well, you could still get married and let your husband take you away. You know you can't hardly make anything working. I'll bet there's no job you could get here that would pay more than two or three dollars a week."

She continued, "Now if you marry someone like Mr. Washburn, someone with a good job, not some dirty miner, you're set for life."

"Someone like Mr. Washburn would be too old for me, I think." I'm afraid I muttered. This kind of talk was making me embarrassed.

"Oh, Maude, you are still wet behind the ears. You've spent too much of your life reading. If you had been at the Palmer House where I grew up, you'd know you're looking at the wrong figures. You're thinking, 'Mr. Washburn is twenty-four years old.' That's the wrong figure to think about. Think, 'Mr. Washburn makes sixty dollars a month.' That's the figure to think about."

I was shocked and must have shown it. I was thinking about that old saying "If you work for money, you work ten hours a day, but if you marry for money, you work twenty-four hours a day."

As though she knew what my thoughts were, Lovey said, "I love Mr. Washburn and all, and I don't care what anyone thinks. It's nice to know a man can take care of you. Besides, this work is easy compared to working for my mother at the Palmer House. At least here I don't have to clean and polish brass spittoons. Mr. Washburn doesn't smoke or chew. He's almost Temperance. It's not so bad, Maude. Mr. Washburn is very nice. He takes a bath once a week, even though he doesn't get dirty like the miners. He's got a good job clerking in the Continental Mine offices. He's got a promise of a better job after a year. He tells me that I'll never want for anything."

"You didn't want for anything at the Palmer House, did you?" I asked.

"No," she said. "But I worked hard. Maw always saw to that. She was always after me, always bossing. Here, in this house, I'm my own boss."

"Will you still be working at the Palmer House now that you're married?" I asked.

"Oh, Lord, no," she said while trying to catch the stray strands of hair and trap them with a hairpin. "Mr.

Washburn wouldn't think of me working. No wife of mine is going to work, he says, like he's thinking of having three or four wives."

I asked if she thought her mother might take me on.

"Oh, yes, indeed. I expect she's missing me right now, although she'd never say so. She's only got Our Annie and Yee right now. If I were you, though, I'd wait until after dinner to go see her. She's always busy right through noontime."

"Is your mother mad at you because you ran off to get married?"

"She was, but she's over it. She knows that Mr. Washburn is a good catch. She gave me that quilt on the bed for a wedding present. It's the Wedding Ring pattern. That's kind of nice. Also, she's going to help pay for the chivaree bill."

"What do you mean, chivaree?" I asked. I was getting all fuddled again. Lovey went too fast for me.

"You didn't hear it last night? What a racket! Mr. Washburn's friends at the Fire Company got it up. They waited until we blew out the lamp and went to bed. Then they made enough noise right outside the house to wake the dead. Singing and banging on pans. We put our coats over our nightclothes and went on the porch. They had us there. They wouldn't let us put on any other clothes except our shoes. They made me sit on a white mule and Mr. Washburn had to lead it. They put a garland around my neck. It was really Christmas chains of paper loops and popcorn. I felt that foolish, I know I blushed beet-red. I didn't even get a chance to put my hair up."

Lovey paused while I tried to picture all this. Scarce

34

two weeks ago, Lovey never had her hair up. It was long and shiny, and she said it was her best feature.

"So, you're on the mule, then what?"

"Well, they led us on parade up and down Main Street until everyone was awake and popping out of their houses to follow along. The women brought lanterns, and some of the men carried pine torches. Even though I felt like a fool, I had the best seat for observing. We went to the Mercantile. The women and children stayed in the store, and each person got a soda. Mr. Washburn went with the men to the Mercantile Bar and stood them all to a drink. So, it added up to quite a sum. Almost the whole town was there. I wish you had heard the noise and come over, Maude."

I know she was sincere, Mama. In her way, Lovey is probably as lonely as I am. She's married so she can't act silly like a girl anymore. But she's so much younger than the other married women, what could they find to talk about?

She put a couple of sticks of kindling in the stove and began to peel potatoes. "Mr. Washburn likes his dinner on the dot," she said.

I didn't know the time had run on so until I saw her looking at a windup clock on the shelf beside the stove. I wasn't planning on staying for dinner even if I should be invited, which I knew I wasn't because she only put two potatoes in the pot. So, I hurried to finish what I had come to say.

"Lovey, will you speak a good word to your mother about me? I'd be that thankful if you would."

"You mean you still want to work at the Palmer House after what I just said? Well, sure. I'll speak to Maw. You

35

go over this afternoon to see her. She'll probably take you on. Probably want you to live there, too, so you'll be at her beck and call. Maw thinks the Devil makes work for idle hands."

"Lovey," I said, "somehow, I have to earn enough money to leave here. I want to . . ." I stopped and looked around. All of a sudden, I felt ears pressed in close, wanting to hear and laugh at what I was going to say. I got Lovey to say she wouldn't repeat it or laugh at me. When I told her I wanted to go to school and learn to be an artist, she laughed at me anyway.

"You can't," she whooped. Then she lowered her voice to a more ladylike level. "I mean, my dear girl, what are you thinking? There aren't any women artists. You'll only make yourself miserable trying to be something God never intended you to be."

"God or something is always pushing me to carve a stick of wood or sketch with a piece of charcoal. Why should God push me to do this if he didn't want me to learn how to do it right?"

Lovey's eyes checked the clock again. "Oh, Lord, I'd better hurry." She unwrapped a square of bacon and sliced several strips. They went into an iron skillet on the back of the sheet-metal stove.

I hurried to get on my sweater and jacket and say my good-byes. That bacon smelled so good. It's been so long since I ate bacon that my mouth was slavering like some old dog's.

With my stomach so empty, Mama, I can see that Lovey makes some sense when she advises me to marry a man who could take care of me.

✿ ✿ ✿

Well, Mama, after I left Lovey's, I went over to Main
Street to the Mercantile Store. There I found another
bitter pill to swallow.

Since I knew Da used to run a bill at the Mercantile,
I stopped in to see about getting a new pair of boots.
Before I present myself to the Palmer House, I'd like to
have boots that don't show my bare toes. I thought Mr.
Willis might let me charge them and pay them off later.

I reckon everyone was home eating dinner. The street
was nigh deserted. I hoped the store would be empty.
It was a painful thing which I had worked myself up to
do.

Several horses were tied in front of the Mercantile
Store and Bar. All of them had the O-X brand from the
Tic-Tac-Toe Ranch. The store is always dark as a cave.
There's only the light from the dirty window and the
open door. Mr. Willis and another man were sitting on
nail kegs near the door, with a checkerboard on a keg
between them. Another man, a cowboy, lounged with
one elbow on the counter watching them.

When I came in, Mr. Willis stood up quick, like I
caught him doing something he shouldn't have been

doing. He tipped his bowler hat and smoothed out his long white apron. I haven't been in the store for some time, so I suppose, with my back to the light, he took me for a grown-up. I have grown. I'm tall enough now to look him in the eye. Which is what I tried to do. It is hard to look someone in the eye when you're fixing to ask them for a favor that involves money.

"Mr. Willis," I said, "do you remember me? I'm Sean Brannigan's daughter, Maude."

He slumped into his apron. "What're you doing here at this hour?" he asked.

I stammered, not knowing what his question meant.

"You know the two hours between noon and two o'clock is set aside so the soiled doves can do their shopping." His arms were akimbo, and he looked very severe.

"Gray doves? Shopping?" I asked, not understanding.

"Not gray doves. Soiled doves. They have a time set aside, and everyone knows it. Decent women should keep off the streets then. You shouldn't be out at this time," he scolded. Then he added, for no reason that I could tell, "And your poor mother scarce cold in her grave."

Mama, then I knew what he was talking about, and I reddened like a turkey's wattle. By soiled doves, he meant those bad women who live along Peacock Gulch and sell their bodies to men. A long time ago, Lovey told me that the Bible calls them whores.

Even though my face was still burning, I pulled my backbone straight and fixed my eye on him again. "No, sir, I did not know of such a thing," I said.

I continued, being very polite and businesslike, saying just as I rehearsed it, "Mr. Willis, would it be possible for you to extend me credit for a pair of shoes?"

"What? What? Speak up," he purely roared at me. I guess I almost whispered because I was so embarrassed.

After clearing my throat, I repeated my question.

Mr. Willis didn't smile. He looked down at my worn-out boots. On the left one, the sole has ripped away from the top and it's like a mouth open to scoop up every pebble and twig in my path. "Wait," he grunted and stuck the chewed-up end of his cigar in his mouth. He went behind the counter, opened the drawer of the cash register making bells ring, and got out a handful of papers.

While I waited, my heart settled down and my face cooled. I looked in the glass cabinet to see if the box of crayons was still there. It was. Now, I thought, if no one buys it, I may soon have it. A job, money of my own, and I can buy crayons and maybe even oil paints without a by-your-leave from anyone.

Mr. Willis bent over the counter doing some calculating on the papers in his hand. He straightened up, shaking his head. "Maggie, this is more a matter that concerns your paw. You might ask him to stop by to see me."

"What seems to be the problem, sir?" I tried to sound as grown-up as possible.

"Well, your father has run up a bill, Maggie, that needs taking care of before I can let you have any more credit."

"Mr. Willis, my name is Maude. May I see those bills, please?"

"This is for your paw to take care of," he said, sounding like he was digging in for a spell of stubbornness.

"My father is not in Eldorado, Mr. Willis." I thought fast, and I thought a little lie might be justified. "He was called away suddenly. He left on a Sunday. You were closed then, so he didn't have a chance to settle up. Now, may I see those bills?"

Mr. Willis shoved them across the counter to me. Some were sort of wilted-looking. Many were from the Mercantile Bar. My heart sank. Da had been charging everything, including my Christmas hat. I could understand the beans and flour and safety matches. But I couldn't understand how he could charge so much liquor. The only thing I can conclude, Mama, is that he took your leaving so hard that he tried to make himself feel better by drinking.

Events were hammering me right into the ground. I seized on small things, details, to think about so I wouldn't burst out bawling like a crybaby. "Let me see your figuring," I said.

He shoved his pencil and scrap of paper across the counter to me. I just made myself concentrate. Slowly I checked his figures, then I rechecked. His sum was too low by five dollars. I found the total to be one hundred twenty-one dollars. I checked again, while he folded his arms, then unfolded them, then put his hands in his pockets. "I'm afraid you've made an error, Mr. Willis," I said, sliding the papers and pencil back to him.

He tried it again. "By hooky, I did. It's more than what I wrote down. I made the mistake in your favor." He fairly crowed, like he had me there.

"Yes, Mr. Willis. It's one hundred twenty-one dollars, I believe."

"I let your paw get in too deep. When's he coming back?"

That was not a question I was prepared for. Before I could stammer out an answer, Mr. Willis bellowed, "He went off to the Yukon, didn't he? Him and Rab. Just like they been talking about ever since the strike up there. They lit out of here and left you holding the bag, didn't they?"

My face was burning again. Trying hard to hold my temper and my tongue, I stuck my chin up and said, "No, Mr. Willis. He did not leave me holding the bag, as you say. He left me property to take care of these bills. I have the papers on my father's claim and our house, and I've got a bill of sale for the cow. So I can settle with you right now."

"Your paw's claim is all worked out. It's no good. That's why he sneaked out of here."

"He did not sneak out of here, Mr. Willis," I said. I was blazing mad by this time. "My family is honest. We pay our debts. I'm trying right now to be honest with you." I stopped talking and bit my lips. I was so mad I was trembling. If I were a man, I wouldn't let this blackguard get away with these insults.

The cowboy standing by the counter must have been listening the whole while. Very slowly, but in a deep, raspy voice, he said, "Let up, Cosmo. She's right. She was honest enough about that mistake she caught you in. Give her a chance."

Mr. Willis looked at the cowboy and then looked

41

down. "I can't do nothing for her, Mr. Collins. That claim is worked out, and everyone knows they are just squatting over there by the trail. That land belongs to the Continental. As for a cow, Mr. Collins, I'm not in the livestock business. Seems that's more in your line." Mr. Willis gave a little coughing laugh.

Mama, I was that humiliated. I felt like dying right on the spot. Squatters. Calling us squatters when I had Da's papers giving me the property. He was saying the very roof over my head wasn't mine. Not trusting myself to speak further, I tried to step around the cowboy, to head for the door.

This man who was called Mr. Collins stood up straight, which put him right in my path. By way of being polite, he lifted his hat just a fraction off his head and let it settle back. "Miss Maude," he said, real polite, "if I could just have a word with you before you rush off."

I stopped and looked up at him. A fair face he had, with steady blue eyes, sort of squinted up. He wasn't as old as Da, but he looked like he knew how to deal with things. I waited in silence.

"I am in the livestock business, like Cosmo says. You reckon I could buy that cow from you?"

I didn't know what to say. Everyone knows ranchers don't keep milk cows.

Finally, I said, "She's not worth much now, I guess. She's dry. She'll have to have a calf and freshen before she gives more milk."

"Well, how about I buy her for one hundred twenty-one dollars and you pay Cosmo here, and he throws in a new pair of shoes for you?"

Mr. Willis was grinning like the cat that ate the cream. "Yeah, that'd be okay, Mr. Collins," he said.

"It's not all right with me," I said. "You've never even seen the cow and you're offering one hundred twenty-one dollars for her. She'd have to be made of solid gold to be worth that much. Do you take me for a fool?"

I turned to Mr. Willis, who again had a scowl on his face. "As for you, Mr. Willis," I said, "I'll pay you when I can. The Brannigans are honest people. We take no charity from any man."

Mama, I couldn't stand any more. I rushed from the store, almost bumping the cowboy in my flight. My eyes were so filled with tears that I could scarce see as I stumbled down the path to the creek. I hid in the cottonwood thicket and cried and cried. It seems I have been handed an awful bitter cup to drink.

Tuesday evening, January 19, 1897

This whole day, excepting the time I spent with Lovey, was a day of mortification and humiliation. Today it was borne in on me how bad off I am. The world seems set against me because I'm poor, female, and young.

To pick up where I left off, I was miserable after my childish fit of crying in the cottonwoods. I knew I had to see Mrs. Steckler at the Palmer House as soon as possible. I need a job as soon as I can find one. I don't have two pennies to rub together. Also, there's the debt to be paid at the Mercantile. No matter how miserable I felt, I had to go ask for a job.

Mama, I don't want to complain. For all I know you've got problems yourself. But I could have used some help today.

In the grove of trees, I stooped down to the creek to splash some water on my face. While I was hunkered down, this big hog — a monster he was — snorted up against me. He almost knocked me over. I stood up fast. He was standing on my skirt so it tore at the waist. That was your second-best, Mama. You probably wouldn't recognize it now. Using a piece of baling wire I tried to pin it back together. As best I could, I washed off the dirt where the hog had walked on me. As I say, I tried to look decent, but I didn't succeed, as I'm going to tell you about now.

As you remember, the Palmer House stands there at the corner of Main and Gold, the biggest building in camp if you don't count the mill.

The sun glinted off the corrugated roof. The false front was peaked against the bright sky. The lettering that says Palmer House, Eldorado, New Mexico Territory, est. 1882 has faded considerable.

I'd only been inside twice before when I came to sell butter for the kitchen. Those times I used the kitchen door. Today, I figured I was there on grown-up business, so I went right in the front door as bold as brass.

Once inside, in the waiting room I guess you'd call it, I stood stock-still. The room was beautiful. I didn't have time to take in everything, but there was a stamped metal ceiling and wallpaper on the walls. It was a real pretty pattern with pink roses going up a kind of trellis. On the floors, rugs, Oriental probably, dark wine color with blues and pinks in flower patterns and fringe on the ends. My fingers twitched to touch the thin carved legs of the little tables. On the tables were coal oil lamps with roses painted on the shades. On a table in the middle of the room, on a crocheted doily, sat a silver bowl filled with fruit that looked like it was straight out of *The Arabian Nights*.

There was no one in the room, so I tried to get my fill of looking. I took in a big sniff of air, too. I sorted out tobacco smoke and an oily smell from the lamps. Then the awfulest stench rose up right beside me. I

45

looked down at my feet. Mama, I had scooped up a load of pig droppings in that left boot.

I started to back out the door so as not to get any of that stuff on the rugs. Before I could get out, the door opposite opened. Lovey's mother came in.

Mama, as I remember, you never met Mrs. Steckler, so I'll just describe her a little. You might not be able to see or hear her where you are. You need to know all this to know how awful I felt.

Mrs. Steckler has a form like those women in the catalogues — swelled out in the top and swelled out in the bottom and almost vanished at the waist from being laced in her corset so tight. She was wearing a beautiful blue dress with sleeves that puffed out big at the shoulders. Her hair was frizzled on top and around her face.

I had a good chance to observe her because, seeing me, she stopped and tilted her head back to line me up in her spectacles. She looked me up and down like I was a side of beef she was going to buy.

Not daring to move for fear of smearing the pig filth on the carpet, I just stood there like a lump on a log. Or like a side of beef.

With her head still thrown back, she started a smile. "Maude. It's Maude, isn't it? Lovey said . . ." She had been moving toward me, but she stopped and sniffed. Almost like a dog sampling the air, she sniffed again. "My Lord," she said, "what is that stink? Did you bring that with you, Maude?"

I was so humiliated I couldn't say a word. I couldn't explain about the hog or not having wood to heat water to wash. I was too shamed to mention Da's debt and

46

me with no way to buy shoes or clothes. I knew I didn't belong in this beautiful room with this woman whose dress was clean and well fitted. Why would she give me a job in her clean boardinghouse? From what she could see of me, she must think that I would ruin all her fine things.

She backed up a piece so she was farther from me. Her voice easily carried. It comes from way down in her chest and sounds like gravel being washed through a rocker.

Even though I was silent, my stomach wasn't. It started a slow burble like stew cooking on the back of the stove. The noise changed to a constant complaint. Then from my gut came loud shrieks like cats yowling at night.

Mrs. Steckler couldn't help but take notice. She backed farther away, frowning and sniffing.

"Maude, I hold myself to be a Christian woman. As God is my witness, I hate to say a thing like this to another human being. But go get cleaned up. You do have soap, don't you?"

I nodded miserably. She was absolutely right. I had about as much business standing on her fine carpets as any of the hogs that wander the streets.

"I'm sorry, ma'am," I managed to stammer. "But I came about a job. Lovey said you might take me on."

"Maude, you go home and get cleaned up. Then we'll talk about a job. Remember, cleanliness is next to godliness."

"Yes, ma'am," I said. She was coming toward me now like she might have in mind to throw me out.

47

I opened the door and scuttled onto the porch. As I pulled the door to, I could feel the pressure of her hand on the other side. I felt she might be cleaning the doorknob where I had touched it.

Through the door, I heard her voice. "Come back tomorrow and come to the back door."

I got home as fast as I could, going across lots instead of following the streets and trails. My stomach kept time with my steps, complaining all the way. I've been hungry all day, but I'm trying not to pay any attention. I've got only a couple of bowls of beans left and three biscuits. I'm trying to stretch them out as far as they'll go. I don't know if Mrs. Steckler is going to hire me or not. Maybe I can't get clean enough to suit her. Maybe she won't want me living under her roof and eating at her table.

Well, Mama, I know you're here. As discouraged as I am with myself, I can just hear you saying, "Don't quit. Keep trying." The miserable have no other medicine, but only hope, as the Bard said.

So, I cleaned my shoes until the leather was slippery from being wet. Having no others to put on, I got the canvas pannier from the roof and cut it into two pieces. With some of Daisy's hay for lining, I tied these on my feet like crude moccasins.

Hot water was my biggest need. There was plenty of water in the spring, and I had a tub and bucket. The problem was wood. Or lack of wood. All around, as far as you can see, the trees have been cut down. On the slopes of the hills, some stumps still stand. But on the claims and building lots, they've been grubbed out. If there was any wood worth burning, it's been gathered long ago and carted off for the smelters or stoves.

Mrs. Steckler didn't say, "No. No job." I have to keep reminding myself of this. "Maude," I thought, "just try to forget the shame, put it behind you. Get yourself clean so you can go there tomorrow and hold your head up."

I was just fixing to fetch water for washing, although it is awful hard to make a lather in it with my yellow soap when it is so cold. Neither did I mush relish the idea of putting my head into that cold spring water to wash my hair.

Then a thought hit me like a clap of thunder. I know where there's plenty of hot water. The hot springs. Where the miners go to soak the grime out of them. Geronimo Springs. You remember, Mama. You said the Indians used them, too. Before the whites drove them out of these mountains. You said they'd camp there until their wounds healed and their sick got well.

It's too late to go today. It'll be about a two-hour walk. As I recall, women and girls get their turn in the mornings and men take theirs in the afternoon and evening.

I'll be ready to leave here at sunup. We'll be ready to leave, I mean. Daisy and me. It's going to be hard to give her up. I'll take her with me tomorrow, so maybe she'll get her fill of grass to eat. Maybe I made a mistake not selling her to that cowboy in the Mercantile. I'm too poor to be proud. That will bear some thinking about. How proud can you afford to be if you're down to bare bottom?

Thursday morning, January 21, 1897

Mama, you've been patient with my fears and complaints. Now I want to tell you about yesterday. There is a puzzle, too, but I'll come to that in good time.

Yesterday was a strange, almost happy day. It was like reading a somber book where everything is gloomy and hopeless. Then in a turn of the page, the sun is shining, the terror is gone, and the page is filled with hope. I must not get swept away, Mama. My plight is still the same. But it is tempting to believe that the day is darkest before the dawn and that my dawn is beginning.

Even the weather was misplaced — a warm, promising spring day stuck into the cold pages of winter. The sun was so bright and the air so clear that I could see dried agave stalks on the mountains to the north outlined as though with India ink. Patches of snow sparkled like gems.

Daisy and I started early and stayed to the trail along the creek. Three hunters on horseback passed us before we were out of the camp, but not another soul did we see on the trail.

Daisy doesn't like being a beast of burden, but she

must earn her way. We bumped along together, me in my hay-stuffed footwear and Daisy with the wash, bucket, and tub rigged to her bony back.

When I got out of earshot of the camp, I thought for a moment I had gone mad. But it was just the absence of the stamping mill thump-thump that left a void in my head. I was cast loose from the rhythm that seems to dictate my heartbeat and footsteps. Oh, how I long to live all my days without that infernal pounding.

After the creek empties into the river, the land opens out into grassy river bottom. Three steers with the O-X brand threw their heads up with a crazy rolling of the eyes and bolted across the river.

Geronimo Springs is just a little way past the mouth of the creek. There was a sign nailed to a pine right by the trail, just as I remembered. It said ladies use the spring in the morning, gents in the afternoon. By the foot of the cliff was the stone bathhouse. Ladies' undergarments were spread on big rocks and draped over bushes. In a cottonwood grove, I saw a buggy and tethered horse.

I staked out Daisy in a patch of grass and took her load off before I satisfied my curiosity about the other users of the spring. Sitting by the river where the flow from the hot spring runs in was a Chinese woman. She had a little fire going with a tea kettle on. She saw me, I guess, but she didn't give any sign.

The bathhouse was next to the rock-lined pool. A pipe was rigged to carry water from the spring into the pool. The overflow drains and runs down to the river in a shallow stream.

I wanted to take off as many of my clothes as possible so I could put all the wash to soak while I bathed. I had sooner undressed in the warm sun, but I could see there was someone else in the pool. So, I went into the cold bathhouse and stripped down to my shift.

Using hot water from a pipe on the far side of the bathhouse, I set my wash to soaking. With my feet tender from their winter confinement in shoes, I limped across the cold smooth rocks toward the pool.

A thin veil of vapor hung just above the water. When I left off watching my steps and stole quick looks at the pool, I saw the head, no more, of a woman. Her wet hair was plastered down on her head and neck and spread into the water like a silky scarf. She was watching me and smiling.

The water was very hot. It probably seemed more so to me because I've not felt hot water these many weeks. At first I sat on the edge and put my feet in. Then I slipped my whole body into the pool at the end farthest from the spring.

Now I was looking at close range into dark brown eyes with eyelashes clotted with water. Amused, she seemed, in a grown-up way. But, I swear, she was no older than I.

"Hot," I said, although there was no need. She smiled more.

"Hello," I said, "my name's Maude Brannigan. I don't believe we've met."

This amused her very much. Whether she was contrasting my formal way of talking with the sight I must have made hobbling into this clearing in my hay-stuffed moccasins, or whether she was by nature a merry person, I couldn't tell. But she smiled a radiant smile. Her teeth were a trifle crooked. Other than that, she was beautiful. At first, I thought she was Mexican because of her dark eyes and hair. But the Mexican women don't look straight at you with that mocking smile. They drop their eyes.

"I'm Venus Adonna," she said.

"Oh," I said. The name took me aback. I put my head back to wet my hair. I tried to imagine a mother looking at her wrinkled, red-faced newborn and saying, "I see that you are going to be a beautiful woman. I'm going to name you Venus for the goddess of love." I couldn't imagine this picture. So I asked, "Is that your real name?"

She laughed again, her laugh seeming both practiced and unrestrained. "What's in a name? That which we call a rose by any other name would smell as sweet." She might have been declaiming on a stage. Her mouth was rounded and her voice well modulated. Her puckered hand lifted from the water to gesture, and I could see she was buck naked.

Mama, I know I looked shocked. The mocking look came back in her face. I've got to get used to looking at the human body if I'm going to be a painter. But I've never seen another naked human except you and me, Mama. And I don't linger long in looking at myself only to see what changes Nature is working on me to turn me into a woman.

So as not to appear completely unworldly, I carefully kept my eyes on her face and said, "Shakespeare, isn't it?"

"Yes," she said, "*Romeo and Juliet*. I've memorized

53

almost all of Juliet's part. I'm going to be an actress."
When she said this she raised her chin and looked defiant, like she was just daring me to laugh. It was the way I felt when I told Lovey I was going to be a painter.

"Like Sarah Bernhardt?"

"Yes. The Divine Sarah. Someday they'll call me the Divine Venus. Or maybe they'll call me the Divine Something Else. I've not completely decided on my stage name yet."

Mama, I could see she might have what it takes to be an actress. Her dark brows came down as she became a woman deciding on her stage name. Her drama was too big to be seen close up. If she were on a stage and I in the audience, it would have been just right.

"Do you know Shakespeare?" she asked me.

I told her how your set of Shakespeare volumes and the Bible was almost all we had to read during your last year.

"I've been reading and memorizing Shakespeare since I was a child. If a person can act Shakespeare, it seems to me, she should be able to act anything."

"You're not more than a child now," I said boldly. "How old are you? I'll bet you were born the same year I was."

With that she stood up in the pool, with the water coming only to her knees. Her skin glistened pearly pink. I was shocked and amazed. She did not look like a child.

I don't have words to say how she looked. But the words that came first to mind were from the Bible, from the Song of Solomon. Joints of thy thighs like jewels; navel like a round goblet; belly like a heap of wheat.

These words never made sense to me before, but now I understood why the writer of that Song said, "How fair and how pleasant are thou, O love, for delights!"

Now I understood the words to mean that Solomon looked on the woman's body as being like all the beautiful and delightful things he could think of. Of course, he was a man, and I guess he would see more of delight in a woman's body than I'll ever be able to see. Though if I'm going to be an artist, I must be able to appreciate the beautiful in men and women.

Venus was so natural, like she was fully clothed and stepping around the horse droppings on Main Street. Not cowering behind crossed hands or being coy with lowered eyes, she stepped out onto the round, dry rocks like the first Venus being born from the sea. I never saw the like before. Then she smiled down on me that mocking smile.

She took so long to answer my taunting question about her age that I wished I hadn't said anything.

"I'm old enough," she said. "Old enough. 'There was a star danc'd, and under that was I born.' *Much Ado About Nothing.*"

She was a strange one, sure enough. Where did she fit into Eldorado? Could she be the daughter of a rancher from upriver? She had not gone to the school during the two years I went. I had not seen her around the camp. All the time I washed my hair and scrubbed my body under the shift, I wondered about her.

The sun was warm and the white clothes spread on the bushes would be drying fast. I didn't want her to leave until I got to talk with her again.

Venus put on a ruffled petticoat, dazzling white in

the sun, and draped a towel around her shoulders. Sitting on a rock downstream from the pool, she put her feet into the water, still warm as it ran to the river. Leaning forward, with her long hair flowing between her spread knees, she would separate a strand, comb it, and throw it back over her shoulder.

When I had soaked all the ground-in grit from under my fingernails and from my heels, I stood up. The shift clung to me, and I realized I didn't leave myself anything dry to put on. I would catch my death of cold if I tried to scrub my wash while I was dripping wet.

Venus threw her hair back to look at me and seemed to know my predicament right away. "I brought a wrapper," she said. "You can use it."

"Hey, Fay. Take this to missy, okay?" Venus held a pink garment out to the Chinese woman. This woman, although smaller than either Venus or me, was older. I don't know how old. I can't tell with grown-ups, especially foreigners. She rose slowly and brought me the wrapper, never looking at me.

I went into the bathhouse to change. Even if they were both women, I was not bold enough to show my nakedness in front of them.

Scrubbing my wash in a hurry, and getting everything spread on rocks, I took occasion for a good look at their laundry. There must be several women in the family. There were different sizes of women's undergarments. I didn't see any men's things at all.

After I had done I sat near to Venus and commenced to comb out my hair, which you remember, Mama, is a difficult task. As soon as I comb out one hank, it curls back on itself and tangles again.

"Do you use anything on your hair?" Venus asked.

"What do you mean? Like soap?"

"No." She explained, "Some women boil out walnut hulls and put that juice on their hair to take out the red color. You know men don't like a woman with red hair?"

"No, I didn't know that," I said. I have never given much thought to pleasing anyone except you and Da, and you liked me the way I am.

"Some women use lemon juice or dry their hair in the sun to bleach it out. Of course, lemons are awful hard to come by in this godforsaken place."

"Do you live right in Eldorado?" I asked, trying to place her.

"Yup. Right in Eldorado," she said.

I was silent, thinking. Having a buggy and a Chinese woman to do the work, she must be a daughter of one of the mine managers.

Venus used a little rock to rub calluses off her feet, and I copied her practice. Across her nose she dabbed a white ointment. "You know you can sunburn your skin even in January?" She handed me the little pot, then looked at me and said, "It's too late for you. You're not taking care of your skin. You're as weathered as the cowboys."

I looked at my hands, red and rough below white wrists, and had to agree with her.

Her hands were smooth and looked like they never scrubbed or worked at all. With a little stick, she pushed on the flesh around her fingernails and made them look nice. She showed me how to do this, although my flesh wasn't soft but was cut and stuck out like dry thorns from my fingers.

"You've got more tricks about beauty than one of those women's magazines," I said.

"Yup. I've got to take care of my looks. Maybe my face will be my fortune." She laughed. She acted like what she said was a little bold. "Just as soon as I have enough money," she continued, "I'm lighting out of here. I'm going to St. Louis and then New York. I can't stand this place."

"But right here is beautiful."

"I don't mean right here. I mean Eldorado, with all that dirt and mud and the stamping mill forever pounding away."

"Yes," I said. "I feel the same way. You know, another thing I hate is the gold fever. These men, they come from everywhere, live miserable lives, and end up with nothing. Then they hear of the next gold strike, and they run to it — even if it's to the ends of the earth."

"Maybe women get gold fever for other things. I think they should follow their fever instead of always trailing after some man."

"Well, I didn't go with my father," I said. I explained how he was a miner and went off to the Yukon.

"You're on your own, then?"

"I've got to be finding a job right soon. I'm hoping to be taken on at the Palmer House. I've got to earn some money so I can leave here, too."

"Are you going to wear those clumps of hay on your feet when you work at the Palmer House?" I looked at her face to see if she was mocking me. I know she's a lot richer than I am, but there's no reason to mock a body, just because she's poor. Venus was serious.

58

"I've got shoes. I'm just saving them."

Venus put her foot beside mine in the water. Next to hers, mine was long and narrow.

The Chinese woman sat in the pool. As the sun climbed higher, my stomach began to rumble. I moved Daisy and got out the one biscuit I had brought with me. When I went back to sit down, Venus was unpacking a basket that sat by the fire. Though my hunger made my mouth water to think of wolfing down that biscuit myself, I remembered my upbringing and offered her half.

"I was just going to offer you some of our lunch. We've got way too much for two people."

Venus poured two cups of tea from the pot beside the fire and handed one to me. Then she brought the basket and put it between the rocks we sat on.

Mama, I'm ashamed to say I was almost reduced to tears by her generosity and the sight of so much food. Sugar for the tea, yeast bread, butter and jam, hard-boiled eggs.

To slow myself down so I didn't act as starved as I felt, I made conversation.

"Where in the world do you get eggs in the dead of winter? I didn't think hens laid in the winter," I said.

"Oh, I don't know. Our cook gets them. We never seem to lack for anything on the table," she said, sounding like someone who never goes near the kitchen.

After we finished eating, my stomach was so excited that it rumbled quite a bit. I walked around picking through the round river rocks, looking for quartz pebbles. I found an odd-shaped little oval stone. Taking a chunk of charcoal from the ashes of an old fire, I drew a little owl face and body on it.

I gave it to Venus. She smiled and her eyes opened wide. "How nice," she said.

"I want to be an artist," I told her.

"We'll both be famous," she said. "Maude Brannigan, the artist, and Venus Adonna, the actress."

"You're the first person who didn't tell me there aren't any women artists and I can't be one."

"You can be an artist — don't forget this is eighteen ninety-seven. We're almost in the twentieth century. Times are changing. Soon women will have the vote. They'll be able to do all the things men do now."

"It would be nice to work at a job and earn as much money as men do. Do you know that a man who works in the Continental Mine office makes sixty dollars a month? I think a woman could work one of those letter-writing machines as well as a man. Then she could earn as much."

Venus stared at me across her white-smeared nose and cheeks. She made a discouraged mouth. "I don't think so. In big cities, I've read, there are women who operate those machines. But they make barely enough to live on."

"It's not fair," I said.

"No, but men run the world, and you've got to find the best way you can to get what you want from the small corner of the world that's not important enough for them to bother with."

Venus said lots of things like this during the time we talked. I was surprised that someone who was that young should have learned so much about the world. Somehow, I had thought that girls who were raised in rich homes would be more innocent than I — would be more sheltered from the world. But, Mama, talking with her was so interesting, it wasn't until afterward that I remembered that I hadn't asked where her father worked or what street she lived on. So, I don't know any more about that kind of fact than what I've just told you.

My wash was still damp, but I got it into a bundle and got myself dressed. I wanted to leave by noon in case any men should be coming to use the hot springs.

Venus offered me a ride in the buggy, but I could see there wasn't enough room for me and my stuff. So I thanked her and rigged up Daisy for the walk home.

The buggy passed before I got far, Venus driving, and Fay holding a big basket of wash steady in back of the seat. Daisy and I stood to the side, and Venus, looking very proper in black skirt and jacket and wide-brimmed hat, saluted us with her whip.

Mama, what a mystery she is. I'm sure she's near my age yet she doesn't seem to have any doubts about how to take hold of her life and run it. Maybe that's what comes of having money. But there's another mystery. If she does have money, why is she saving it to leave and be an actress?

Sunday, January 24, 1897

Mama, I hope I haven't lost you because I moved and I didn't have time to write. I didn't forget you, but I've not had time to sit and reach out for your presence. Too much else presses in. It is only now, late on Sunday afternoon, that I have time — and so much to write about, too.

I probably need your guidance more here, Mama, than I did when I lived alone in the soddy. In this new world filled with people, I see that I'm very unworldly and not really prepared to live as a grown-up. But I intend to keep my mouth shut and learn as much as I can. I fear that I may be thrown among rascals and be taken advantage of before I know the way to deal with them. I've moved into a life in which I'm a stranger. So, bear with me, Mama.

When I came back from Geronimo Springs, with myself so clean — I must have washed off a ton of dirt — I felt I was a stranger in the soddy. When I lifted the pallet to put the clean sheet back on it, a black beetle crawled from a crack in the earth wall. Its armor was lustrous and cleverly hinged at the legs. Not afraid of me, he lumbered across the pallet as though taking possession. My visit to the springs must have cleaned my eyes, too, for now I saw how miserable and dark the soddy was. I could see this burrow in the hillside was a more fit home for the beetles and other wild creatures than it was for humans.

I took Daisy and my bill of sale to the feed store. Mr. Hurley took her in payment of the bill. I'm square with him and have one less burden on my mind. Daisy will get plenty to eat while she's there.

Daisy was my last link with our old life. You and Da gone, then Daisy. Now when I earn enough, I'll leave here, too.

And I do have a job. After I traded off Daisy, I went on to the Palmer House and went to the kitchen door. Yee, the Chinese cook, let me in. He either keeps his eyes down all the time or he was staring at my boots. I looked at his high forehead and little square white cap perched on top of his head. They say all Chinese men have long pigtails so they can be snatched up into Heaven when they die. If Yee has one, it's under his cap. Our Annie was working in the kitchen, too. She gave no sign that she knew I was there.

The smell of beans cooking was so powerful, my mouth just juiced up. I worked at standing still, waiting for Mrs. Steckler. Feeling virtuously clean and proud of restraining my hunger, I stood as tall as I could. When she came through the door and saw me, she stopped dead in her tracks and sniffed, then sniffed again. Apparently, I passed that test, but she appeared to be frowning about my appearance as she got near me.

"Well," she said, "Maude, you're back." Reaching

up, she took me by the shoulder and turned me around like I was some kind of doll. Already, before I ever had a job, I was beginning to see why Da doesn't like to work for a boss.

My clothes were in rags, but they were clean. My boots were falling apart, but I had tied a bit of leather strap around the left one so I wouldn't scoop up anything else in it. Mrs. Steckler sniffed some more. Then she seemed to make up her mind.

"I'll put you on as a hired girl for three dollars a week, room, and board. I'll treat you as one of my own, but I expect you to work like one of my own. Just like Our Annie here," she said, motioning to the Indian girl in the corner of the kitchen. The landlady rattled this out in her gravelly voice.

I thought of Lovey, who didn't like being one of Mrs. Steckler's own. Then I thought of the three dollars a week. It would take a long time to pay off Da's debt, but the board sounded good. At least, I wouldn't be slavering from hunger like I was at that very moment. There was naught I could do but accept and be grateful that she'd take me.

"Yes, ma'am. I'll work hard. When do you want me to move in?"

"Right now will do. Come with me. I'll show you your room."

She led me outside, and we followed the porch that ran around three sides of the house until we came to an outdoor stairway to a landing on the second level. From the landing, a door opened onto a long hall. With the outside door closed, the hall was dark and musty smelling. Mrs. Steckler opened the door on the right and motioned me in.

My new home is very elegant, maybe like your girlhood home in Virginia, Mama. It's a small room with the roof slanting so that I have to watch my head when I walk near the outside wall. But set into a dormer is a dear little window with white lace curtains and white window blind. What a blessing to have one's own window onto the world. At night I can look out at the stars. I'm attracted to a special constellation — Orion with his big shield.

The bedstead has little iron vines curling around the ironwork and is a bit short, but I can tell you after four nights of sleeping in it catty-corner, I make myself very comfortable. There's a washstand with a pitcher and washbasin and a cotton towel hanging on a rack at the side. The mirror above the basin is wavery so you can make your eyes look big or little by raising up and sinking down.

Mrs. Steckler could see how happy I was with the room. She spoke severely, like she wasn't going to have any hired girl being happy around her place. "I expect this room to look exactly like this on the day you leave," she said. "Right across the hall is Our Annie's room. Not that she'll be much company to you. She doesn't talk, you know."

I started to ask about Our Annie, but I didn't get a chance. When Mrs. Steckler talks, she sounds like a cannonball rolling down a long washboard and she doesn't stop until she gets to the end of her thought.

"There's no one else up here on the second floor. Just

you and Our Annie. Business is way off. The Palmer House used to be full all the time. Turned visitors away. But Eldorado is going downhill. People are moving down to Santa Cecilia since the silver strike there. Just like Tombstone. I was there in its heyday. Georgetown, same way. These mining camps grow like mushrooms. Then it's over and everyone's gone. I guess I ought to think about moving on, too. Maybe Canada." She stopped and sighed. "But I'm slowing down and . . . Well, I won't burden you with my troubles. Do you need help moving your goods?"

"Yes, ma'am. If it's not too much trouble. I've got a trunk and a pot or two is about all."

"Stop by Drayage and tell Rollie I said to move you. Move in now and I'll put you to work in the morning. You'll eat in the kitchen with Our Annie and Yee. You'll work every day and have time off Sunday morning for church and after Sunday dinner you can tend to your own affairs."

As an afterthought, she said, "Are you keeping company with anyone?"

My cheeks went hot when I said, "No, ma'am."

"Just as well. Girls get married these days while they're still wet behind the ears. By the time they've learned some sense, it's too late."

I wasted no time going by the Drayage, then running back to the soddy. Even though my muslin ceiling had got soot and water stains on it, I took it down, folded it carefully, and put it in the trunk with my other stuff. Your picture may be smoked-up, but I can see enough to remind me of how you looked.

66

Immediately, without the muslin ceiling, dust and small stones began sifting down from the roof as strings of burros loaded with wood came down the trail jarring rocks loose. Since I'm trying to stay as clean as Mrs. Steckler expects me to, I dragged my trunk outside and shook myself off.

I wired the bed frame across the door, but I expect I'm giving the house back to the beetles and other critters that lived there before we did.

After four days of living on the Main Street side of Eldorado, I feel as though I'm a whole world away from life in the soddy. There is traffic of horses and ore wagons, with the drivers geeing and hawing like the animals are deaf. At night, noise from the saloons gets pretty loud. During the day, there is always coming and going with people greeting each other and standing on the boardwalk to talk. There's those little boys that should be in school, but aren't, with their loud swearing and yelling of "You old hoss, you" at each other. In back of it all, reminding me that I haven't come so far after all, is the thump-thump of the stamping mill.

The Mexicans from Chihuahua Hill and the Cornish from Pine Flats keep to themselves most of the time, but they do their shopping in the Mercantile. In the afternoon, I've even seen a buggy with the soiled doves from Peacock Gulch go by for their appointed time at the store.

I've kept my eye open for Venus Adonna. I've been too busy to engage in small talk with anyone, so I've not even asked where the Adonna family lives. She remains as much a mystery as ever.

67

At first, every passing buggy caught my eye, but I learned the hard way to control my attention. I was in the kitchen pouring bacon drippings into the stone jar where they're stored when I heard several horsemen go by. While I was gawking at them, I poured the drippings down the front of the long white apron that Mrs. Steckler gave me to wear.

When she saw the mess I had made, she kept asking the Lord in a loud voice to give her Christian forbearance. He must not have heard her because she bawled me out and called me a ninny to boot. And she was right I'm ashamed to say. She's not paying me for looking out windows.

In the dining room, where Mrs. Steckler is training me to serve table, I got into more trouble. Mrs. Steckler says there are rules, or maybe they're laws, about how everything should go — the knives, forks, spoons, and napkins. Now this is all a lot of foofaraw as far as I can tell. There is one long table, laid with a white cloth, with places set according to Mrs. Steckler's laws. The men — almost all the customers are men — scrape back the chairs and hoist themselves up to the table. Inside of a minute the utensils are every which way, the napkins are tucked into their collars or lying on the floor, and they're wiping their mouths on their sleeves.

Be that as it may, Mrs. Steckler was very displeased when I took the napkins out of the little metal or wood rings they were in and folded them beside the plates. "Were you raised in a barn?" she growled at me. "Everyone knows a man puts his napkin in his own napkin ring so he's sure of getting the same napkin next time at table. It's the sanitary way to do things. It's taken me long enough to get these uncivilized miners trained. Now you're trying to undo it." She went on in that vein and then assured me that if she weren't a Christian woman, she couldn't abide all these tribulations.

I just say, "Yes, ma'am," and try to look meek. But I do get riled sometimes. As you know, I'm not used to being spoke to in such a fashion.

I'm glad she's Christian, too. If she didn't have the restraints, modest though they be, of Christianity to hold her back, I don't know what violence she'd be capable of.

Trying to avoid her tongue-lashings, and not wishing to call her attention to mistakes on my part, I did practice deceit yesterday.

I had been sent to the parlor, for that is what the grand room in the front is called, the one I thought was a waiting room. My job was to fetch the lamps back to the kitchen, where I would clean the shades, trim the wicks, and fill the bowls.

I wanted to look at all the pretties in the room, but I couldn't keep my eyes off that bowl of fruit. There was one apple, one banana, one pear, a cluster of grapes, and an orange. They glowed like they had some kind of light inside. Each was most natural-looking, but so perfect as to look unnatural. The very perfection added to the temptation. I had never touched an orange before, so I held this one in my hand and felt the goose bumps on its skin and the little nib on the end where it had been fastened to a tree.

Mama, I swear, all thought of Mrs. Steckler and jobs

and responsibility went out of my head. I must bite into that forbidden fruit, and I did. Just as soon as my teeth closed, I knew I had been a fool. The orange was made of wax. There I stood with the waxy bite in my mouth feeling like Eve when she got tricked.

"In for a lamb, in for a sheep," I thought. With the fruit hidden in my apron pocket, I made for the kitchen. Only Yee was there, sitting at the worktable looking for rocks in the dry beans scattered on the table. I couldn't very well ask him to leave the kitchen, so I just took my chances that he wouldn't tattle on me.

The wax softened as I held it over the stove. I stuck the bite back into the orange and smoothed it over. Warming it again, I pressed the dishrag against the surface to make the dimples.

When I finished and looked at it, I couldn't see the mend and I think I've got a good eye. I smiled, and for the first time, Yee smiled, too. I winked at him and ran to the parlor to get that orange out of my possession as soon as I could.

For giving way to temptations like that, I was purely ashamed. As I will tell you when I write more later, temptation looms about me every day.

Monday, January 25, 1897

Mama, as I ended before, I was speaking of temptations and I will continue. As you will see, I'm sore tempted and need your help. Either help me to resist or tell me that it's all right to give in.

These tales of temptation somewhat concern Our Annie and Yee, so you must first know something of them.

Because of Lovey, I'd known about Our Annie but hadn't paid much attention when I was younger. Now, I recalled what Lovey had said. Our Annie is full-blooded Indian — Apache — and was taken into the Steckler home when she was about two years old. No one knows exactly how old she is because she was brought in by hunters who found her. She was the last survivor of an Apache family that hid out in the Mogollon Mountains.

As her Christian duty, Mrs. Steckler took the little heathen to raise. Our Annie was already in the family when Lovey was born. They played together like any sisters until time for Lovey to go to school. Then their lives took separate paths. Lovey made friends with white kids from school, and Our Annie went her silent way as a sort of slavey in the various boarding houses that Mrs. Steckler ran. I say "silent" because she's never talked. Lovey said, "No one knows why. We know she isn't deaf. Maw wouldn't waste money paying a doctor to examine an Indian."

When I first showed up at the kitchen door and Yee let me in, Our Annie was ironing. From under the window where she had the board set up, she'd cross the kitchen to the stove. Snap. Out came the cold iron so it could reheat. Snap. The handle clamped onto a hot iron and she was back at the ironing board. She didn't look at anyone and seemed to be in a world alone. Without a change of expression or any puckering up of her brows, she worked the sadiron in and out of the ruffles on a petticoat. The only noise from her was the sizzle of the spit on her finger as she tested the hotness of the irons.

It's hard to describe how black hair can be, but hers is a black that makes Da's hair look washed-out. It hangs in a long braid down her back. She dresses much the same as I do, in a white shirtwaist and a black skirt. Her clothes are not raggedy like mine. Of course, she is short and her face is round like a child's. Since she has been with Stecklers for fourteen years she must be close to sixteen. Just think, Mama, she's got no real memories or experience of being an Indian, yet she's always been treated like one.

She must have heard, as I have, people saying, "A good Indian is a dead Indian" and "Kill the pups, like you do wolf pups." Does she know, I wonder, that people hereabouts still dread an Apache attack? It is many years since Geronimo was caught and Mangas Coloradas was killed, but the army still keeps troops at the fort in Santa Cecilia.

You can't hardly blame one young girl for all the massacres Apaches did. What does she think?

Even though her room is across the hall and we pass as we go about our duties, I haven't tried to speak with her but once.

You see, Mama, on my first night here, I came up the outside steps carrying a bucket of hot water to wash up before I went to bed. (Mrs. Steckler reminds me constantly that cleanliness is next to godliness, and sniffs at me like she expects to catch me smelling like a pigsty again.) My door has no lock, only an inside latch, so I shoved it open with my elbow and went in.

Just inside the door, I stumbled over something and almost spilled my water. After I lighted my lamp, I saw a pair of women's shoes sitting just inside the door. Nice black shoes with buttons up the side, almost new, hardly soiled on the soles. I didn't know what to make of them, but as I examined them I could see they were close to my size. I tried them on, and they're a bit long, but otherwise just right and as stylish as any in the Mercantile. But they can't be mine. So I took them off.

Because no one else is supposed to come up the outside stairs except Our Annie and me, I thought she might know something. With the shoes under my arm and holding my lamp, I stepped across the hall. Just before I tapped on her door, I thought I heard a small voice singing. After I knocked, I waited for a long while, hearing only the soft whisper of clothing being donned.

73

Our Annie opened the door and for the first time looked me in the eye. Her glance didn't last long but slid off over my shoulder.

"Do you know anything about these shoes?" I asked. I know she understood me. She shook her head No. "Who do they belong to?" I asked.

She lowered her head and looked at my stocking feet.

"Do you know how they came to be in my room?"

Another shake of her head, then she slowly closed the door and I heard the bolt slide.

So, Mama, another temptation. Can I believe these shoes are meant for me? Not many women have feet so long as mine.

These shoes make the same problem for me as the food does. The food is so abundant, and I'm still so hungry, that I just want to grab with both hands and fill my mouth. So it is with the shoes. I need new ones so much that I was tempted to just wear these without trying to find out who they belong to. Who would give me shoes? I'm no Cinderella. I've no fairy godmother to give me shoes.

You, Mama, are the only one looking after my welfare, and I know you can do that only in a spiritual sense.

But, wait, Mama. As I think this through, I believe Yee may have told me the answer to the mystery.

On the morning after I found the shoes I went early into the kitchen wearing my old boots with the leather strap holding on the left sole.

Yee looked down at my shoes and said, "Missy's boot smiles." I thought he was being inscrutable the way Celestials are said to be.

"Um," I answered.

"Missy need new shoes," he said. By this time he was shaking down the ashes in the stove. I could scarce hear him, but I think he said, "Wear new shoes."

At the time, I thought I didn't hear him right. The hired help here don't express their thoughts too well. Our Annie doesn't try at all. Yee speaks in short bursts of words. Often he covers them over with cooking noises. I suppose I'm afflicted, too. When I do speak, I look over my shoulder to see if Mrs. Steckler is around. It's not that I mind if she hears what I say. She'd not like me talking at all, I know.

No one else has mentioned shoes except Yee. Mama, I feel a nudge from your good sense. "Wear the shoes" is what I'm feeling. It's been these five days now, and no one has claimed them. If someone bawls me out or acts scornful to me because these shoes really belong to them, then I can take them off. Yes, Mama, I know the scorn can be no worse than I've already borne. I know, with your help, I've the strength to bear it.

There is one more thing, Mama. There's a hunger, a yearning, raging through me that's not satisfied by food or shoes. There's no name for it. I feel this thing is savage and I need help in subduing it to my working life. Let me explain by giving an example.

When I was scouring the pots and pans, I saw Yee start to put a stick of kindling in the stove. This unreasoning force I'm telling you about made me forget what I was doing or where I was. For in that piece of wood, hidden in the knots and swirling fibers, I saw Our Annie.

75

So I grabbed the wood from Yee's hands. I suppose it scared him some, but I didn't pay attention to anything as I groped under my apron for my knife in my pocket. The wood was soft pine and easy to cut. I had scarce started before the neat part in Our Annie's hair came alive under my fingers. Then her round face with her eyes looking at something she was holding in her arms.

So intent was I on what I was doing, and Yee, too, I think, was watching so hard, we didn't know Mrs. Steckler had come into the kitchen.

"So this is how you waste your time when I'm not around," she bellowed. My hands were still curled around where the wood had been, so fast had she snatched it from me and thrown it in the fire. "If you want to be idle, you can join those no-good whittlers sitting in front of the Fire House all day while decent people work."

I turned away from her so she wouldn't see my tears. Yes, I was angry at her. But more, I was sad because I'd never see what Our Annie was holding in her arms.

Mama, I know you encouraged me to be what you called "artistic," and I know I want to be an artist. But I can't be one now. I have to get away from Eldorado first. This force doesn't have any patience. It wants to burst from me right now. Mama, this ferocity that compels me to grab a piece of wood and start carving is not helping me here. My only way out of Eldorado is to stick to the straight and narrow path laid out for me by Mrs. Steckler.

Mama, please help me.

Wednesday, January 27, 1897

Mama, this part of my life is so lovely, the part after I've done all my chores and I come to my room. The lamp casts a golden glow bright enough to read or write by. After washing up and getting ready for bed, I read for a while in our little Shakespeare volume, the play of *Coriolanus*. Without your help, I can't make much sense of it, so I've put it aside to write to you.

The wind rattles the metal roof above my head and whistles around the window casing. Still, with a blanket wrapped around me, I'm cozy. It's been a week since I moved in, and I've got the hang of things. Now that I'm getting my strength back, I'm not tired all the time.

Having whole shoes on my feet makes me feel better, too. I thought everyone would be looking at my feet in the new shoes, but the only one to comment was Yee. Yee looked at my feet and said, "Missy's foot not smile." Yee may actually have smiled when he said this.

To damp some of my yearning to draw or carve, I brought a piece of kindling to my room with me last night. From it, I carved a tassel-eared squirrel. He was holding a ponderosa pine cone in his paws, looking for all the world like someone eating an ear of corn. He is a pretty little fellow, even though I can't smooth him as I would like. My soul benefits, I think, from my making things with my hands.

I wondered if a look at the squirrel might not provoke a smile from Our Annie. I crossed the hall and knocked on her door. She opened it, but held it so she could close it fast if she had need to. Before she could move, I held the squirrel out to her, right close to her white shirtwaist so she would know that I meant for her to take it. She lowered her eyes to look at it, then lifted it from my hand so delicately that I didn't feel her flesh. Without another look into my face, she closed the door softly. There was silence in the dark hall. The bolt was not rammed into place.

I came back to my room and sat down to write to you. In a matter of minutes, there was a gentle tapping on my door. I jumped to open it before my visitor changed her mind and fled. Our Annie stood there looking down at her open palm. She thrust it toward me. On it lay three paper circlets with gold and red designs on them — bands from cigars.

Little children pick these up from the street and keep them with their treasures. I felt very honored that Our Annie wanted to give me something that was valuable to her. Without taking the cigar bands, I stepped back a pace to draw her into the room. Maybe, now that the ice was broken, I could get Our Annie to talk to me. Showing more shyness than fear, she came into the room. I took the cigar bands and put them on my fingers the way kids do.

"Thank you, Annie," I said. Then I held out my hand

to admire it as though I were wearing diamonds and emeralds.

She turned to go, but I said, "Wait, Annie. I want to show you something." I rushed to my trunk and threw the lid back. On top of my goods is the folded muslin with your picture on it, Mama. I unfolded enough to show Our Annie your likeness. "This is my mama," I said. "She's gone to be with the angels in Heaven. Is your mother in Heaven?"

Our Annie looked at the muslin and then back at me, her face round and solemn and her eyes shining like black shoe buttons. At first her face was blank. Then her mouth turned up in the smallest of smiles. The barest murmur, just a whisper, came from her lips. "Mama," she said.

Mama, I was so moved that tears came to my eyes. The first sound I heard from this young savage slavey was the word that I hold so precious. I hope, Mama, that your spirit was in this room to share the excitement and hope.

Our Annie seemed overcome by a fit of shyness. She ducked her head and darted out of my room and into her own.

This morning, after breakfast was done and all my morning work finished, she and I arrived back in the kitchen about the same time. Our Annie put on her coat and got a broom, dustpan, and bucket from the pantry.

Then she looked at me and did an odd thing. She jerked her head, like she was trying to tell me something. A second time, she did the same motion and held the bucket out to me.

Yee, who was watching, said, "Our Annie want Missy go to bar. Go with Our Annie."

"Our Annie goes to the bar?" I asked.

"Our Annie cleans bar. You go."

"But Mrs. Steckler . . ." I said.

"Is okay. You go."

I put on my coat and took the bucket. Our Annie led me to the back side of the Centennial Bar, where a small door was set into the board and batten siding. She unlocked it, and we went through a storeroom and into the bar.

I have never been in a bar before, but the idea has always had an attraction. I suppose that's because only men and wicked women go in them and because Da and Uncle Rab were always so merry when they had been to one. But going into this empty one spoiled the attraction. The stale-beer and cigar-smoke stink was enough to make a pig gag.

In addition to being sickened by the stink, I couldn't believe the dirt. The potbellied stove was running over with ashes and spotted with spit from men aiming at the coals and missing. The sawdust on the floor was stained with spilled beer and tobacco juice. Around the spittoons was a mess worse than any made by an animal.

Our Annie had not brought me here to see the dirt, though. She had something else in mind. Shoving and nudging, she got me in front of the bar and then pointed.

Above the bar was a picture of a naked woman. She was stretched out on a divan and was near as long as the bar itself. A painting was what it was. An oil painting. I stepped behind the bar and gawked at the rosy flesh, at the blue-eyed face skewed at a funny angle on the head. Her face, shoulders, and bosom faced out, but her stomach, hips, and legs were from the side. It looked an uncomfortable posture. The woman's hands were folded across the place where her legs come together. I didn't count, but I think she might have too many fingers. But I stared and stared, seeing how the paint was brushed on. As you know, Mama, I'd never seen an oil painting before. But how I want to paint one, now that I see how it's done.

Our Annie was standing close, watching. Her face had a glow like she was struggling with some inner feeling.

"I've never seen anything like this, Annie. Thank you for bringing me," I said. Encouraged by the way she was watching me, I smiled broadly. I plucked from my skirt pocket a small carving of a snail, a carving I hadn't yet finished. "This is for you when I'm done with it," I said.

For just an instant, she smiled and her lips formed some word. I could swear she said, "Thanks." As fast as it happened, it was over and she was back in her own silent, expressionless world.

I grabbed a broom and started sweeping up the sawdust and putting it in the bucket. Our Annie busied herself with other cleaning.

As I started out back to dump the sawdust on the trash pile, Our Annie stopped me. She held a gunny sack and motioned me to pour the sawdust in it. This I did.

As we worked together, I talked. It's somewhat like

81

talking to you, Mama. I'd say a mouthful, then look at her. No audible response. If Our Annie had her back to me, she didn't turn to look. But there's something that tells me she's listening and undertsanding. I have to guess at what she'd say if she said anything.

I said, "How come you clean the bar? This is a filthy mess. Does Mrs. Steckler send you over here? I wonder what her connection is with the bar? I never thought about who owns it. Surely not Mrs. Steckler, her being Christian and Temperance and all."

No response.

"Mrs. Steckler is one woman who makes her way in a man's world. Where is Mr. Steckler? I've never seen him."

Our Annie picked up empty bottles from behind the bar.

"There are not many ways a woman can earn her own way in the world. You could run a boarding house, or teach, or nurse. In a city you could be a type writer. I want to be an artist. Everyone says there aren't any woman artists."

Our Annie whisked a cloth up and down the bar until the heavy varnish gleamed.

"I suppose you could say the soiled doves earn their own way, too." I took another good look at the oil painting. That woman was a soiled dove, I guess. What else was she doing naked in a bar?

"When you know the choices, you see that Mrs. Steckler is doing all right. Maybe she has to be sharp-tongued to stay in her business."

After chewing that over in my mind, I said, "Maybe I just ought to put being an artist out of my head. Seems

82

like I'm fighting the whole world. Look how things have come around in just the week since I came to Palmer House. In return for letting someone else decide how I spend my time, I have a very nice room and I'm well fed. I even have new shoes. And tomorrow is payday. I'll have money — money I've earned to begin paying down the debt at the Mercantile."

Our Annie was not making any clatter as she cleaned. More and more she watched my face.

"You don't get paid, do you?" I asked suddenly.

In answer, her hand twitched at the black skirt. "Clothes," I thought. "She's saying she gets paid in clothes."

A current of understanding flowed through my brain. Our Annie doesn't have anyone to talk with any more than I did after you were gone, Mama. Most likely, she hasn't had anyone since Lovey started school so many years ago.

In her head, she could be making comparisons between her and me. What hopes does she have? What chance of being anything but a stranger in the white man's world? Now, after all this time, she'd probably be a stranger in the Apache world, too.

"Can you read and write, Annie?" I asked.

But I'd gabbed long enough. The noon whistle blew. We threw on our coats, grabbed our cleaning stuff, and ran. Just before Our Annie locked the door, she seemed to remember something. Back inside she went and came out carrying the gunny sack with the stinking sawdust in it. We hightailed it back to the boarding house to get there before the men came for dinner.

Tonight after my chores, I brought some brown wrapping paper and a stub of a pencil to the room with me. From memory, I tried to sketch the oil painting I saw in the bar. It didn't come out.

So, I closed my eyes and remembered Venus at Geronimo Springs. I tried to draw her. There's lots I don't know about drawing. Her picture came out smudged and stiff with none of Venus's life in it.

Maybe I am foolish, Mama, in not just shutting this hungering to draw and carve out of my life. Maybe I should just do like Lovey did and use common sense instead of giving in to this yearning to do something with my hands. On this Main Street side of Eldorado, I've got to decide how I want my life to go.

Sunday afternoon, January 31, 1897

Mama, this day was so full of troubling events, I scarce know where to start.

I will mention Thursday when I got paid. With three dollars in my hand, the first money I had ever earned, I felt rich for a few minutes. I ran over to the Mercantile, planning on paying the entire amount against our bill there.

Remember those temptations that I told you about? No sooner had I entered the store than another temptation blossomed right before my eyes. In a glass case was that box of crayons, waiting there since my last visit. That brought me up short. Faster than it takes to tell about it, I had bought the crayons and a tablet of drawing paper for one dollar. That left two dollars to apply to the debt.

Well, one hundred twenty-one dollars take away two is one hundred nineteen dollars. I guess it is something to have paid that much. Still, my conscience digs at me that I didn't have the willpower to resist the crayons.

On the other side of things, it is sheer pleasure to roll the red crayon real light over the paper and get a blush-pink and build it up gradually so that I have all shades of red.

85

I have resolved that on my next payday, I will be quite stern with myself and put all my pay against the debt.

Now for Sunday dinner, which I have just finished cleaning up from. On Sundays, lots more people come than we have for weekday dinner. Some women come, and most people are wearing their churchgoing clothes. There's less rushing and more lingering and talking. After dinner, Mrs. Steckler even lets the guests sit in the parlor.

Most of the time during the week the men talk about mining: Someone's high-grading the ore, silver sells for such and such, they're taking such and such amounts of gold out of some mine in Colorado. On Sunday, the conversation is on a higher plane and I might learn something of the world if I could just draw a chair up to the table and sit down to listen.

But I'm in and out. First bringing in the big platters and bowls of food. Mrs. Steckler goes whole hog on Sundays. Venison saddle and roast turkey and ham. Mashed potatoes and biscuits. And beans. We always have a pot of beans. Mrs. Steckler says some miners won't sit down to a table that doesn't have beans on it.

I hear, "What Bryan meant was . . ." and I'm out of the dining room and into the kitchen to get the water pitcher. When I return and go around the long table filling everyone's glass, I hear, "When Mr. McKinley takes office . . ." As I move on, it's "Gladstone told the English people . . ." Then, I guess these miners never let mining get very far out of their minds for I hear, "Piece of float, a nugget worth about thirty-four dollars." "That was in South Africa, you say?" "New tele-

phone, as soon as we get the generator to working."
"Imagine that. Electricity right here in Eldorado."

Yes, Mama, there are a variety of people, many well educated, that sit down at our table. On Sunday, Mr. Collins of the Tic-Tac-Toe Ranch, the very same who witnessed my humiliation at the Mercantile, was there. He watched me, but I took no notice, it taking all of my attention to keep that long table supplied with victuals.

Lovey and her husband, Mr. Washburn, sat next to him. Squeezed in among the regulars was a man, a stranger to me, whose manners and clothes made him stand out. I heard someone asking him about the territorial government in Santa Fe. He, replying with a laugh, said that one couldn't keep up with the twists and turns of the politicians there.

Miss Katy was there. You remember Miss Katherine Gynne, the schoolteacher? She was wearing a suit of light green velvet and I just wanted so much to touch her shoulder to feel of the goods. She turned and looked up at me as I served. "How are you, Maude?" she asked. I guess she had heard I was working there because she didn't seem surprised to see me. Seated between her dad and the Santa Fe man, she turned frequently to talk to him. Most of the miners and cowboys fall to their food in complete silence and don't say a word until they've sopped the last of the gravy off their plates with a piece of bread. Miss Katy's voice could be heard quite clearly. "A school, you say? In Santa Fe?" she asked.

"Yes, Miss Gynne. Right in the Palace of the Governors. We set our easels up and work in the big front room. The Santa Fe light is very inspiring for an artist.

Perhaps when your school is not in session, Miss Gynne, you'd like to attend a painting class or a sketching class."

"Oh, I think not, Mr. Jennings. I can hardly draw a straight line," Miss Katy said. She laughed a breathy laugh I had never heard in the classroom.

"Now it's an art teacher you are, Mr. Jennings?" I heard Mrs. Steckler's booming voice ask from her end of the table. She went on, "I thought you said you were a sign painter." There was a scornful note in Mrs. Steckler's voice, like she thought the painter was passing himself off for something he wasn't and it was her job to set the record straight.

Mr. Jennings didn't seem bothered. He cut his meat carefully and chewed slowly. I noticed he put his knife down when he talked instead of sitting there with a knife in one hand and a fork in the other just daring his food to try to escape. "If you want to earn your way in the West, Mrs. Steckler, you have to have more than one string to your bow."

By this time I could slow down a little, so with my tray under my arm, I just stood by the kitchen door watching and listening. Mr. Jennings was an artist. Mr. Jennings painted. Mr. Jennings taught art in Santa Fe.

While I was watching him closely to see how an artist was different from other people, I heard my name. Mrs. Steckler's voice roared, ". . . ought to get acquainted with Our Maude here. She fancies herself to be an artist."

Everyone at the table stared at me. Feeling myself go hot and red, I turned and dashed through the door to the kitchen. How did Mrs. Steckler know? She must have ransacked through my room to see my sketches. I never left my things out on the table, but always put them away in the trunk. I was so confused and angry, I almost didn't notice that I had become "Our Maude" just like "Our Annie."

Still, embarrassed or not, I wanted to talk with that man, the one Miss Katy called Mr. Jennings. I heard a scraping of chairs being shoved away from the table and I slipped back into the dining room.

There was a general mixing and crowding as the people stood and moved toward the parlor or the door to the porch. I slipped through the crowd until I was almost touching Miss Katy's dress.

All at once, I felt hands around my waist. Someone was behind me, and the fingers were sliding up toward my bosom. (This is shameful to write, even if there's no one to see it but you, Mama.)

Without pause, I turned and jerked loose. I slammed my tray into the stomach of a youngish man. He bent, with both hands holding his middle now instead of mine. With his face pushed against my ear, he snarled, "You wait, Miss High-and-Mighty. I'm going to take care of you."

Mama, at that moment, I did not even know his name. Whatever gave him the idea that he could take indecent liberties with me, I don't know. But, apparently no one was aware of what he had done. The crowd cleared a little circle around us and he slunk away still holding his belly. I was left to be the object of their open-mouthed stares.

Mrs. Steckler bellowed, "Maude, whatever do you mean by such behavior?" She shoved me through the kitchen door and continued her bellowing. "Business is bad enough without you hitting the paying customers. Flem is a regular Sunday customer. Why did you hit him?"

I tried to explain about his touching me. "He probably just brushed you accidentally. And if he did feel you, you were probably asking for it. How do I know what you're up to? I can't watch you all the time."

That made me feel guilty, but the only thing I had really done to feel guilty about was biting into the wax orange. I protested. "It was no accident. He deliberately tried to shame me in front of everyone."

"So, if he did, no harm done. You'd best get off your high horse, young miss. You're just a hired girl here, and no better than you should be, if you ask me."

Well, Mama, I have to get over my anger because I have to continue to work here. But I do feel dirty that a creature like that man should make free to put his hands on me. It seems Da might have the proper idea about a girl needing to be under the protection of a man. I was certainly mistaken in believing that I would be under Mrs. Steckler's protection at the Palmer House.

There is a scratching at my door. Maybe Our Annie?

Sunday evening, January 31, 1897

Mama, it was Lovey that was scratching at the door when last I was writing to you.

"Come on downstairs," she whispered. "Let's get a cup of coffee in the kitchen. Mr. Washburn went down to the Fire Company for a meeting of some kind."

As I followed her down the outside steps, she still whispered. Mrs. Steckler was taking her afternoon nap and Lovey didn't want to wake her.

Yee was in the kitchen, making up some sourdough bread, but Lovey ignored him. Many girdles of dried leather-jacket beans hung from nails in the rafters. I got down a couple of strings to work on. As we sat at the table and talked, I split the hulls with my thumb and dumped the beans into a bowl.

Since I started working, I haven't seen Lovey to talk to. She looked even more married than when I went to her house. The thought still foremost in my mind was my anger at her mother's ill treatment of me, so I kept quiet rather than have that spew from my mouth.

After a few remarks, she finally asked, "What happened in the dining room? Why did you hit Flem?"

"Because he had his hands on me in an indecent way," I answered.

"You mean . . ." She stopped, taking note, I guess, of my indignant look. "He probably just likes you and is too ignorant to know what to say."

"Likes me? He doesn't know me from Adam's off ox."

"Maybe you should get to know him. They say he's found a good vein of ore over on the west side of the mountain. If the Continental buys him out, he'll have a small fortune."

"He's disgusting, Lovey. Do you know what he said after I hit him? He said 'I'm going to take care of you.' I'm afraid now."

"You shouldn't be," Lovey said. She grinned at me like she was brushing away the seriousness of Flem's threat. "Someone else is interested in you. Guess," she commanded.

"Oh, Lovey. No guessing. That's for little kids. What are you trying to tell me?"

"Well, Mr. Washburn says that when the men all went out on the porch after dinner, Cody Collins pushed Flem into the street. He told Flem that he thought he should take his meals someplace else, not at the Palmer House."

Lovey grinned triumphantly. My face got hot, and I knew I was blushing. I remembered Mr. Collins in the Mercantile trying to buy my cow and to pay me much more than she was worth. Today his eyes followed me as I served at the table. I didn't tell any of this to Lovey. She was already too satisfied with her news.

"Don't be silly, Lovey. Why would an older gentleman like Mr. Collins be interested in me?" I asked. I kept my eyes down, and even my own ears told me that I sounded sweet and simpering.

"Because unmarried females are scarce around here," Lovey said in her matter-of-fact way.

She added, "Remember what I told you about the wrong numbers. You're thinking age, which is no more than thirty-four or thirty-five. Think numbers of acres. Think numbers of cattle. Mr. Washburn heard that Mr. Collins has a contract to supply beef to both the army post at Santa Cecilia and the Indian reservation in Arizona. That's thousands of cattle. That's thousands of dollars."

Lovey paused and looked like the cat that ate the cream. "I know something else, too. Cody Collins is going to ask you to the Box Social on Friday next."

"I swear, Lovey," I said, "you're just making things up. That's a silly thing to say."

"No, honest. He's already asked Maw if you can get off work. You must have seen him casting sheep's eyes at you all during dinner."

I said something, but even I couldn't tell what I was muttering. Finally, I said, "Well, I don't have anything to wear. And no money to buy anything."

"Pooh, that's no problem. You can wear one of my . . ." Lovey stopped. She knew this was impossible. I was much taller than she was. She started again. "There's my mother's . . ." We both laughed, thinking of Mrs. Steckler's waistline so small as almost to vanish and my girth like a sturdy oak tree.

"Well, you can buy some goods and make up a dress. The Mercantile will give you credit."

"But, Lovey, I don't want to run up any bills. I'm

93

trying to save money to leave here, not make more debt to keep me here."

"Lordy, you're stubborn. You're going to end up getting married just like all women do. You might as well open your eyes and get a man that'll make you a good living."

"Come up to my room," I said. "I want to show you something."

Upstairs, Lovey drew her thin Sunday shawl closer around her shoulders. "This was my room, you know. Lordy, but it's as cold as it ever was. I guess it evens out, though. In the summer, the sun on that iron roof just bakes the soul out of you."

From the trunk, I took my scraps of drawings and showed them to Lovey. She giggled when she saw the nude drawings.

"See what I want. I want to be an artist. I'm going to leave this dirty, ugly place and go somewhere to study how to do it."

"You mean someplace like Santa Fe to learn from someone like Mr. Jennings?" asked Lovey. She, too, had been listening to the conversation at the dinner table.

"Yes. Something like that."

"If you married Cody Collins, you could hire Mr. Jennings to stay at the ranch to teach you," Lovey said. She was most persuasive in her arguments.

"Oh, Lovey. You just don't want to understand what I'm saying. When a woman gets married, it's a baby every year and working from dawn to dusk. That doesn't leave any time for what she wants to do."

"That's woman's life, isn't it? Always has been, always will be."

"I've got more time to myself right here," I said. "Let's not fuss at each other, Lovey. Sit down here and let me try to sketch you."

"Make me look like one of those ladies in the magazines?"

"Sure. I'll try."

Lovey shook the bed to test its safety. "Have the slats fallen out from under you? They used to fall and land me on the floor. I told Maw those wood boards were too short for the bedstead."

Since the bed made Lovey uneasy, I sat there and she sat by my table.

Lovey sat still for me until the goose bumps rose on her arms. I sketched her with her head bent and an arm resting on the table. With my blue crayon, I shaded around her head, making a light shadow.

"Is that really my likeness?" she asked. She compared the sketch with the wavy image in the mirror. Because she seemed pleased with it, I told her she could have it.

Now that she's gone, I've been thinking on the various things we talked about.

I have to keep reminding myself that Lovey considers herself lucky to be married to Mr. Washburn. She's only wanting me to follow the same path she took when she talks about me marrying Mr. Collins. Or even that disgusting Flem.

What sense would it make to marry someone like that blackguard Flem when I'm afraid of him right now? There's more wickedness in that man than what I've seen so far for him to try to take advantage of an innocent girl. Must I, just because I've no husband or

95

father or brother to stand up for me, allow myself to be treated like any common street monkey? No matter what Mrs. Steckler says, I think not.

As I've read it somewhere, Mother Nature bestows virginity on her children but once. I intend to defend my person fiercely until I've got enough judgment to decide what I want to do and who I want to do it with.

Mama, am I foolish to think I can take care of myself? Or should I encourage Mr. Collins to think I might make a proper ranch wife?

Tuesday, before supper, February 2, 1897

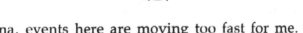

Mama, events here are moving too fast for me. I feel myself being pushed and pulled, to and fro. I scarce know what to think.

On Sunday night Lovey got me all stirred up talking about the Box Social and Mr. Collins. I don't want to go to the Box Social partly because I don't know what's expected of me. Trying to play a grown-up lady is difficult. I'm afraid I'll be a fish out of water. I don't know how to talk to people, politelike. Either I am too silent or I blurt out the first thing that comes to tongue.

Whether I am to go has been taken out of my hands, it seems. Yesterday morning, I was scrubbing the pans after breakfast when Mrs. Steckler swept in. Not one hair was out of place on her freshly frizzed head. A starched white blouse rose from her tightly crimped waist and swelled over her high jutting bosom. A brown brocade skirt draped up at the side, just like the catalogue pictures.

"Maude, may I speak with you?" she asked.

"Yes, ma'am," I said. After I pushed my hair back with my forearm, I wiped my hands on my apron and turned to face her. My white blouse and black skirt could have done with a washing.

"Maude, dear," she said and then frowned. Holding her little finger out, she reached up and lifted a hank of curls from in front of my eyes.

"You must do something about your hair. You're no longer a child, you know."

Silently I waited. I knew Mrs. Steckler didn't call me "dear" and rearrange my curls without a reason.

"Mr. Cody Collins talked with me yesterday. He says he'd be much obliged if I'd let you go with him to the Box Social this Friday night. Mr. Collins is a gentleman. He'll show you the proper respect. I gave my permission. I even told Mr. Collins what little I know of your family — your father and poor mother."

Mrs. Steckler seems to have changed her tune since Sunday. Then I was no better than I should be and it was all right for her customers to take liberties. Today, Mr. Collins should show respect for me.

"Thank you for your interest, Mrs. Steckler," I said, trying to sound as cold as possible. "I'm afraid it's impossible for me to go to the Box Social with Mr. Collins or anyone else."

"What do you mean — impossible?" she said in her gravelly voice. "I told him you'd go — so you're going."

"The only clothes I've got are these you see before you. I can't go out with a gentleman in the same clothes I wear to clean spittoons."

"Is that all that's worrying you? When I was your age . . . Well, just wash and iron that outfit and do something with your hair. You'll be fine. In a hundred years, no one will remember."

One hundred years, I thought, is a long time to live

down the mortification of going to a Box Social looking like a kitchen slavey.

Mrs. Steckler must have taken note of the stubbornness in my face. She added, "Besides, when you're married to Cody Collins, you'll have as many new dresses as you like. He's well off, and he'll be well off even if the mines close. And he'll be in from his ranch on Friday expecting you to be ready. See that you are."

Mama, now there's two of them, Lovey and her mother, going on about me marrying Mr. Collins, just like it's been ordained and I don't have any choice in the matter. I didn't make any reply to her, but I was beginning to dig my heels in.

In midmorning, I went to my room to get my sweater so I could work outdoors. Our porch and walks are thick with mud and I thought to clean them. The second floor was quiet. Our Annie was at the Centennial Bar, doing her daily sweeping out.

When I entered my room, I swear, Mama, I almost staggered back against the door. Spread across my bed was the most beautiful dress I've ever seen. It was light green silk — the green that is the color of Indian paintbrush in the spring before the orangy flowers show. The dress was fitted at the top, with flowing sleeves that didn't look near long enough to cover arms and a long skirt. I was so fascinated that it seemed to me to spill and sparkle like a waterfall. On the floor, right by the dress, sat a pair of kid boots — soft as butter, I found — little buttons up the sides, cream-colored they were.

Now, Mama, as I said before, I know I'm not Cinderella, that some fairy godmother is going to be fixing

99

me up with shoes and clothes and maybe a crystal carriage with six white horses. I was happy enough to get the shoes before, but this is different. I feel like I'm being pushed along the path to marriage. I'm not content to just wear the clothes and be ignorant. I want to know what's going on and who is behind it.

Lovey first came to mind — but Lovey would want to see what I made of such a dress. Lovey wouldn't make it a secret.

Mrs. Steckler was my next guess, but I know, also, she wouldn't make any secret of it. Helping me like that would add stars to her crown in Heaven, but Ruby Steckler wouldn't be satisfied if God was the only one who knew of her charity.

In casting my mind back, I remembered Yee was in the kitchen when Lovey and I talked and when Mrs. Steckler proclaimed to me that I was going to the Box Social. Too, I thought Yee knew something about the first shoes.

I went pell-mell down the stairs and into the kitchen. Yee was stirring something in a pan with his long chopsticks. He works those sticks like tongs and can pick up anything with them.

"Yee, there's a new dress and some shoes in my room. Do you know anything about them?"

He held up a scrap of pork in the chopsticks and poked it toward me. "Taste, Missy. Need salt?"

"Never mind salt, Yee. I asked you a question."

He went back to stirring, his head tilted back and his eyes partly closed — his inscrutable look. At last he said, "I put dress and shoes there."

Even though I suspected him, I wasn't ready for his

answer. I waited. Yee acted like the matter was closed.

"So where did they come from?" I asked.

Yee was embarrassed. There was nothing inscrutable about him now. His frame seemed to shrink inside his miner's overalls. Finally, he said, "Yee say to them, this not work. Get Yee in trouble."

"Who, Yee? What's going on?"

"My woman work at place in Peacock Gulch. They call her Fay."

"Fay? Fay is your wife? Then you know Venus Adonna?"

Before he could answer, the rest of what he said crashed into place in my mind. "Peacock Gulch? You mean where the soiled doves live?"

My eyes must have been as big as saucers at the thought that followed that one. "You mean Venus and Fay are soiled doves?" I couldn't believe it. They looked so respectable when I saw them at Geronimo Springs — all that white linen.

"No, no. Not Fay. She cook, work like me. Missy, she fancy lady."

Well, Mama, she had pulled the wool over my eyes. Quoting Shakespeare and all. I thought she was a lady, and here she was a soiled dove — a fallen woman. I felt like I used to when I was a little child and someone offered me a pretty, then jerked it back before I could take it. When I had bettered my condition, I wanted to find Venus and be friends with her. Now I find that she is not good enough for my friendship. As you know, decent people just don't associate with women in that shameful trade.

That dress upstairs, and the shoes, too, and the very

shoes I stood in had all come from a house of ill repute. My toes started to curl from the disease and sinfulness that might be in those shoes.

"Yee, I can't accept clothes from someone who . . . Well, I just can't take them," I said after I pulled myself together.

He shrugged, I think.

"You'll just have to take them back," I said firmly.

"No. Not Yee. Yee not do. Yee quit. No more carry this, carry that." He rattled pots and pans so ferociously that I could scarce hear.

I could see his point. To take back gifts to Venus would be to throw insults in her face. She had tried to help me. And she tried to do it secretly so that I wouldn't owe anything to her. The honorable thing to do was take them back myself.

But to go to a house of ill repute. To go to Peacock Gulch. I couldn't do that. Even if Mrs. Steckler thought I was no better than I should be, I knew I had a good name to uphold.

"Yee," I shouted, "stop that banging and listen."

"Yee," I said when he quieted down, "how can I see Missy Venus? Not go to her house, but meet her somewhere?"

"Yee fix," he said. He seemed glad to be out from under the burden of secrecy. "Today. After dinner. Miss Boss sleep. You go past Fire House, past school. Wait at bottom Peacock Gulch. Missy drive out with buggy."

Well, Mama, I did just that. You may be sure I felt like I was walking into the jaws of Hell, carrying the Devil's own finery in a clean gunny sack. I will own that

I did not take off the shoes from my feet. I had worn them these many days and did not feel they had imparted any wickedness into my system. Besides, I threw away my old boots and had no others to wear. As the old saying is, if we have to choose between potatoes and principles, we choose potatoes every time. So, I chose those shoes over my principles.

I do not know how Yee got my message to Venus Adonna. But when I arrived at the foot of the Gulch, she was sitting alone in a buggy, waiting for me. Her horse stamped impatiently. She beckoned me to get in. Shaking my head, I motioned her to get out.

Dressed today in a dark blue suit, with white showing at the high neck, her hair pulled up like a lady's, and a little hat with a veil pulled down over one eye, she looked older. Had I made a mistake? Was this the naked girl who shot out of the water at Geronimo Springs like a mermaid? Yes, there was the same mocking smile in the corner of her mouth.

Carefully, holding her skirt high enough to clear the wheel, she descended. With just the tips of her gloved fingers she guided me behind the shack that used to be the assay office. I wanted to jerk my arm away so afraid was I of the sin and disease in her touch.

My face must show every feeling because Venus asked with raised eyebrows, "Have I changed so much since we last met?"

"Well, I found out what you do. I guess that changed the way I think of you," I said. I could see no point in beating about the bush on that subject.

I hurried on with this unpleasant meeting. "I brought

your dress and shoes back. Knowing what I do, I can't wear them." I thrust the gunny sack toward her.

With her hands holding a little pocketbook close to her bosom, she scarce glanced at the sack.

"If that's all that's worrying you," she said, "then there's no problem. You must have noticed that the clothes are too large to fit me. They belonged to someone who doesn't need them anymore. As I can see, you not only need these clothes but more as well."

Even with my face flushing hot, I held my ground. "Whose clothes are they, then?"

"It seemed a shame to let them go to waste or be ruined by those strumpets at the house. They belonged to Big Effie. She was tall and gave a lot of thought to her clothes. She had a shapely figure and looked quite handsome. It took your mind off her face." Venus paused as if she had said something she didn't mean to say.

"Her face? Was she diseased?" I asked. From the Bible I know the wages of sin — those horrible diseases that are passed from father to son, yea, even unto the fifth generation.

"No, no." Venus sounded impatient. "She had her nose bit off in a fight in some cathouse in South Dakota."

Even though I didn't intend to keep the clothes, I kept asking questions. I guess partly I was astonished at this world that existed unknown to me in Eldorado. As far as our soddy was from the wax fruit in the Palmer House, that's how far again the Palmer House was from Peacock Gulch.

"What happened to Big Effie that she doesn't need her clothes anymore?"

"Oh, she's dead. She got shot by some cowboy who was so eager to get his pants off that he forgot to take off his gun belt first." Venus might have been talking about the weather, she was that casual.

I dropped the gunny sack like a hot potato.

"Silly, she wasn't shot in that dress."

"Well, I'm much obliged to you," I said, "but I still can't take these."

"I suppose your boss, Mrs. Steckler, will buy you clothes to wear. She's pushing you at Cody Collins, isn't she?"

"How did she know so much?" I thought. Yee, I suppose.

She looked at the shoes on my feet. "I gave you those, too, you know. I don't see you trying to give them back. You need them too much, don't you?"

Blushing again, I knew she was right.

"I'll pay you for them when I can," I muttered.

"No. I don't want pay. I want you to keep them and use them. Be sensible." She sounded like a much older woman. Again I could see she had much more experience of the world than I did.

She continued, "Mrs. Steckler is never going to pay you enough to buy clothes, though she'll work the life out of you. Our Annie is practically a slave there. Now listen to me. I'm not trying to talk you into my way of life. I just want you to open your eyes."

She lectured on, and I listened meekly. "You and I both have to make our own way. Being a . . . soiled dove was something I knew about. You might say I was born into the profession. That's how I got into it. Now you might think I'm selling my body. I'm not. I'm only

105

renting it. When you get married to someone because he has money, that's selling your body. None of my customers are my masters. As you can see, I make enough money to dress well. I have time to read and improve my mind. And I've got money laid aside for when I leave this life and make my way as an actress."

Venus spoke so well, her voice so quiet and ladylike, that I found her reasoning persuasive. And, Mama, I must confess, I think I warm to her because she is like me. She has ambitions to get away from Eldorado and better herself.

Even though she seemed not to be watching me, she must have summed up my state of mind. More softly she said, "Take the dress. It's just a piece of cloth. Cloth can't be good or bad. Go to the Box Social. Be beautiful. Have a good time. Flirt with your handsome Cody Collins. To step out with a man doesn't mean you have to marry him."

She paused. Then teasing, she said, "You'll lead apes in hell yet."

"What do you mean?" I asked, confused.

"Shakespeare. It's supposed to be a punishment for old maids."

Quickly turning, she left. After a while, I picked up the gunny sack and took it back to my room.

Tuesday, after supper, February 2, 1897

Mama, when I wrote this afternoon, I didn't think I would be putting pencil to paper again tonight. But I must.

My life continues to be full of astonishments. I would not believe this if I did not see it with my own eyes. Venus Adonna showed up in the dining room for supper tonight, just as bold as brass.

As I believe I said, our trade is falling off. Tuesdays are especially slow because that's the day Mrs. Garcia makes enchiladas and almost everyone goes over to Chihuahua Hill to eat at her house. In our dining room there were a couple of cowboys, some miners from Bear Creek, a fellow who works in the office at Continental with Lovey's husband, and, of course, Mrs. Steckler. Even Mr. Jennings was not there. He was off in his rented buggy someplace to the west painting signs on the sides of buildings.

I started serving at 6:00 P.M. on the dot, as usual. Already I had plates in front of everyone and the men had their napkins stuck in their collars or their shirt fronts or thrown on the floor. At the same time as I was returning from the kitchen with a plate of biscuits in one hand and a big bowl of beans in the other, the outside door opened. A man held the door to allow a young black-haired woman to come in, then he lifted her fur-bordered cloak from around her shoulders.

Mama, I, and everyone else in that room just gawked. It was Venus, wearing a long red velvet dress with her shoulders and chest as bare as the day she was born. Her hair was pinned up, and she wore a little ruffled red velvet hat over her right brow. She was so beautiful she could have just stepped out of a fairy tale.

The man — he looked to be an Easterner, a businessman — was going bald on top but had bushy gray hair everywhere else — muttonchop whiskers, eyebrows, and curls around his high collar. He was about the same height as Venus. A big-linked gold chain stretched across his paunch, from one side of his vest to the other.

As he hung their coats and his hat on the hat tree, there was a hurried scraping of chairs as the clerk from Continental Mines and Mrs. Steckler stood up.

"Mr. Turner," she said, rolling her gravelly voice around. "Welcome to Palmer House." She came from her end of the table with her hand out to him.

"Yes, ma'am. Thank you, ma'am." He gave one pump to her hand and let it drop.

"And this must be . . . ?" Mrs. Steckler stared at Venus, and I swear I saw the landlady's nose wrinkling, sniffing the air like a hound on the scent of prey.

The man had his hand in the middle of Venus's back, and his red face beamed at her like she was an especially fine turkey he had brought down. There was something a little uncertain about the man's features, but I didn't catch on until later that he was tipsy.

Venus also had the look of someone showing off a prize. It finally came to me that this was one of the men she rented her body to.

"Yes, this must be . . ." Mr. Turner said.

Before he could say any more, Venus said, "I'm Miss Adonna." She bowed her head in a very ladylike way to Mrs. Steckler. I wondered how anyone so beautiful could be anything so wicked as a soiled dove? I'm afraid, Mama, that I still have much to learn of the world.

Mrs. Steckler seemed to have her doubts, but she turned away abruptly and pulled out two chairs from the table. "Maude, two more places for our guests," she said to me. A grim look settled into her face.

As I turned into the kitchen, I caught Venus watching me with that mocking smile. Maybe she was comparing her line of work with my line of work. Her mouth and cheeks were carmine. Everyone in the room was staring at her except the clerk from Continental. He was still standing and had his eye on Venus's companion.

Disregarding the napkin hanging from the front of his shirt, he stuck out his hand to the older man. "Mr. Turner, I didn't get a chance to meet you when you were in the office this morning. I'm Zachary Long," the clerk said.

"Ah, yes, yes," Mr. Turner said. He acted like he was used to being treated with great respect.

The clerk sat down, but leaned forward to talk past the miner and Venus sitting between him and Mr.

Turner. "Are you planning on being here in Eldorado for a few days, Mr. Turner?"

"Just long enough to write a report for our stockholders back in Denver."

Mrs. Steckler caught my eye and jerked her head toward the kitchen. When I came back with the potatoes and a platter of steak, everyone was silent, buttering biscuits and such. The cowboys and the miners were still gawking at Venus. One miner had buttered his thumb right up to his wrist and had hit the highwater mark where his cleanliness stopped. I worried that he might pop his hand into his mouth and chew it while he was enchanted by Venus.

I ran back to the kitchen again to fill the water pitcher and grab the big coffeepot. As I went around the table filling cups, I breathed in more than the smell of coffee. It was like bending over a kettle with various ingredients brewing in it. The cowboys smelled like leather, sweat, and manure. I knew when they stood up, they'd leave prints of their haunches stamped on the chairs. From the miners came an odor of old, old sweat and dust, and from one, I breathed the sharp scent of blasting powder.

When I was pouring for Venus, I picked up a perfume odor. It was strong, flowerlike, but animallike, too. Also, I smelled the sour smell of wine on her breath. Was this what caused Mrs. Steckler to wrinkle her nose?

When I was close to Mr. Turner, I knew for sure why he had that muzzy look. He had been drinking, too — rotgut, from the raw smell of his breath.

As usual, Mrs. Steckler smelled of vanilla and camphor. I hovered in the dining room, not because I was needed, but out of curiosity to see what would come from these conflicting smells.

One of the miners stopped shoveling in food long enough to say to Venus, "Huh, I didn't expect to see you here, Venus."

"Miss Adonna," Venus snapped, cutting off his nervous giggle. She nibbled at a dainty piece of steak on her fork.

I caught Mrs. Steckler's face. This had not been wasted on her. I'm sure she knew Venus Adonna's profession. Ever so sweetly, Mrs. Steckler said to Mr. Turner, "How disappointing not to see Mrs. Turner with you. I trust Mrs. Turner is well. Such a lovely lady, your wife. Such a Christian."

"Mrs. Turner was unable to come on this trip. She is at present with our married daughter who is due soon." Mr. Turner was intent on wiping up his gravy with a biscuit. He didn't seem to care two figs for Mrs. Steckler's prying questions.

I didn't know what to think. There he sat, a married man, just as bold as you please with a soiled dove by his side, a girl young enough to be his daughter, or even his granddaughter. Maybe they were just friends, I thought. Maybe they're related, and he only takes a fatherly interest in Venus.

"Miss Adonna, I don't believe we've met," Mrs. Steckler said. "Do you live in Eldorado?"

Venus looked so grand that I marveled she was only my age. "Yes, ma'am. I live on the other side of town. I don't often dine out," she said.

"Do you live with your family?" Mrs. Steckler asked.

"Yes, ma'am, in a manner of speaking."

"Your father. What does he do? I don't believe I've heard the name Adonna in Eldorado."

"My father is often called away by business interests elsewhere, ma'am." Venus was only pushing food back and forth on her plate. It was a good thing she wasn't hungry. With Mrs. Steckler firing questions at her like that she didn't have time to chew.

"Do you live on Cornish Hill, then?"

"No, ma'am. I think mostly the Cornish miners live there."

"Adonna is not a Cornish name, then? I don't believe I've heard it before." Mrs. Steckler drew herself up like she was stiffening to do battle. She was smiling, but what she said next was not very friendly. "Is Adonna a Mexican name then? It sounds Mexican to me. You know I don't allow Mexicans to eat here."

Venus's face was ablaze, and her eyes narrowed like a cat's. "I'm no more Mexican than you are, you fat cow. You've gone out of your way to insult me."

Venus jumped up, and her chair fell over backward. She grabbed Mr. Turner's right elbow and he looked a ridiculous sight, trying to get his fork to his mouth while she pulled at his elbow. "Now, my dear," he said. "What's the matter? What agitates you? Let a man eat, can't you."

"Come on, Homer. I want to go. I told you we shouldn't come here. I told you this cow would insult me." Venus didn't sound so grand now. She was screeching and jerking Mr. Turner's arm.

112

"Oh, you strumpet, harlot. You Jezebel. Thinking you could come to my house, a decent house, and flaunt yourself. Think you could pull the wool over my eyes, did you?" Mrs. Steckler's voice was getting louder and was sure to carry the day because her natural tone was like a booming drumbeat.

The men customers swiveled their heads back and forth to take everything in, stuffing their mouths without bothering to look at their plates.

Venus finally got Mr. Turner to his feet. Did he give Mrs. Steckler an apologetic look? I don't think so. He just looked annoyed. After he fumbled in his pocket, he brought out a five-dollar bill and laid it on the table. Venus meanwhile had grabbed her cloak from the hat tree and headed for the door. Her face was crumpled like a little girl's — like she was trying to keep from crying.

Having been myself a victim of Mrs. Steckler's bullying, I knew how she felt. I wanted to say something, do something. I scarce knew what was in my mind as I hurried through the kitchen door. Yee was standing on the other side, close enough to listen, and I almost knocked him over. I dashed from the kitchen and out the back door. It was pretty cold outside, but I didn't put on a wrap — or even notice the cold.

As you know, Mama, Mrs. Steckler has given me occasion to doubt her Christian goodwill. But sometimes, I can see why she does what she does. Like this time, I know that a line must be drawn between decent people and people like Venus who live immoral lives. But I know that a line wouldn't be drawn against Mr.

Turner. If he came by himself to the Palmer House he would be allowed to stay. Yet he is committing the same moral offense as Venus, but with less excuse. Perhaps his offense is the more heinous in that he is committing adultery, which the Ten Commandments forbid. With him, there is less justification, but only the desire for entertainment.

On the other hand, Venus earns her way by what she does and does not become a burden on the community.

I will confess that I did not think all these heavy thoughts until later. I only know that I was scandalized that Mrs. Steckler should drive anyone away from her table when they were doing nothing offensive. Humble though our lives were, Mama, we never refused bread to anyone — Mexicans, Indians, or dirty miners. I think you and Da would not have turned away a fallen woman, either. So maybe that's why I wanted to talk to Venus so that she wouldn't think I was Mrs. Steckler's handmaiden in all things.

I ran around the porch. Mr. Turner was just closing the dining room door behind him. Venus waited on the sidewalk, pulling on her white gloves. "Do hurry, Homer," she said. "What took you so long?"

"Calm down, my dear. I had to pay the good lady."

"Good lady, my foot," Venus said. She seemed on the point of saying more when she saw me.

"Is this Mrs. Steckler's factotum I see before me?" she asked in a cold voice. "Did Mrs. Steckler send you out to further blacken my name?"

Mr. Turner went past her and out the gate. Venus still faced me, looking haughty and hurt at the same time.

Now that I was facing her, I wasn't sure what it was I wanted to say. "Venus, wait. Mrs. Steckler didn't . . . She'd probably fire me. What I wanted, Venus, was to say thanks for the dress. I'm going to do what you said. I'm going to wear it."

Some of the anger went out of her face. Mama, I don't know what came over me, but what I did next, I know I'm going to regret. I said, "Venus, will you let me make a sketch of you? I'd like to get down on paper how you look tonight."

Friday evening, February 5, 1897

Mama, I believe this is the most exciting day of my whole life. I am scrubbed until I gleam, dressed to the nines, and sitting at the little table in my room with my box lunch all ready to go.

It's not yet time for Mr. Collins to call for me to take me to the Box Social. I scarce can sit still and wait. Every sound of horse hoofs prompts me to run to the window.

To calm myself, I write to you. Also, I want to confide to you something I dare not say to a living soul. Mama, I think I'm pretty.

Yes, yes. I know the old sayings "Pretty is as pretty does" and "Beauty is only skin-deep." Maybe those sayings were made up by plain people who don't know how good you can feel if you think you're pretty. And it's not just skin-deep. I feel good to the soles of my dove-colored shoes.

My face is lightly dusted with rice powder, and my hair curls naturally into what Miss Katy says is the latest style. It's held back from my face by an ivory-colored length of lace she gave me. I'm wearing the notorious dress. I can't help but remind myself that the dress has more history than I do.

To keep up my appearance during the evening, I'm to retire from the company of Mr. Collins from time to time and pinch my cheeks and bite my lips to get a red glow.

Lovey and Miss Katy even advised me about the box and the supper for two people that is in it. I covered the box in muslin scraps and drew roses and vines on it. In the kitchen, Yee stood over me and singsonged in Chinese to be sure I cooked the chicken right and made the piecrust flaky. The box is now wrapped in plain butcher paper. Miss Katy says not Mr. Collins nor any other male is to see the box until the auction. I'm only supposed to hint to Mr. Collins what my box looks like so when it's put up to auction, he'll know it's mine and can bid on it. Miss Katy says great hilarity is created when one's beau is trying to buy the wrong box. As I understand the box auction, I may end up sharing my box supper with someone I don't even know, though if it comes right down to it, I can hardly be said to know Mr. Collins.

I'm a Cinderella who has escaped her cinders for this evening. From the kitchen downstairs comes the sound of Yee's pot rattling. Supper is on the table in the dining room. For the first time since I've been at Palmer House, I didn't put it there. Our Annie is doing the honors tonight.

Miss Katy is staying the night at the Palmer House and going to the Social with Mr. Jennings. She asked me to her room downstairs to help her dress, but she helped me far more than I helped her. At first I was shy because I remember her being so strict in school. But she is very kind and much younger than I thought. She's twenty-three years old.

This morning she rode to school with a cunning little trunk fitted behind her saddle. After teaching all day, she came to the Palmer House to get dressed. So, from about 3:30 P.M. we've been working at getting ready. That trunk is like having a genie at your beck and call. It contains an amazing amount of female goods: Miss Katy's lovely ivory georgette dress, combs, brushes, soap, unguents, ointments, powders, hose, shoes, hair curler and hair papers, and even a hand mirror.

First Miss Katy had me try on my fancy dress. I told her the story of it and she just laughed. She said, "Big Effie was better endowed in the bosom than you are, Maude." She showed me how to take in the dress for a better fit.

When I tried it on again, she looked like she was trying to hide a smile. "Maude, you have to leave off that shift. It's not the fashion to have your undergarments sticking out the top of a dress like that."

"But, Miss Katy, my arms and shoulders will be bare," I said. "It's February. I'll catch my death of cold."

The truth was, Mama, when I took off the shift and saw that expanse of white skin, I couldn't bear the thought of eyes looking at my nakedness. I knew I'd feel every gaze to be full of needles.

Miss Katy didn't like the idea of so much nakedness, either. "We need to cover you up here, but not with your shift. It's much too racy-looking for an occasion like a Box Social." She still smiled.

Under her direction, I took a flounce off the bottom

of the skirt and filled in the top with it. Now only my forearms are bare and white. They compare oddly with my red hands, but I can bear with that. They're red and chapped from honest labor.

Miss Katy has a little stick like the one Venus used. She let me use it and showed me how to push back on my fingernails until white half moons showed. Why this is considered more beautiful than no half moon is beyond me.

"Look at these," Miss Katy said, showing me the little white dots on her fingernails. "My grandmother says that's how to tell how many children you're going to have. Three dots, three children."

I laughed because I had stoved a finger against the gate and I had seven marks on it alone and three more on my other nails. "If that's so, then I'll spend most of my life having babies," I said.

"Well, girls get married so young, it's possible. Like Lovey. She's only fourteen, isn't she?"

She continued, "It's because we live on the frontier that there's such pressure on children to grow up fast. It's especially hard on girls because there are so few women here in the Southwest. All the bachelors watch to see when females turn from girls into women. I had my first proposal when I was your age."

"Have you had lots of proposals?" I asked.

"Oh, my, yes."

"And lots of beaux?"

"No, not really. Some of the proposals were in letters from men I didn't even know," she said.

"How about Mr. Jennings? Is he your beau now?"

She smiled and winked at me. "I don't know. I've seen him only once since the Sunday Dad and I met him here at the Palmer House. We'll just have to wait and see about Mr. Jennings."

"Is he a real artist?" I asked.

Miss Katy seemed eager to talk about Mr. Jennings. She said, "Oh, yes. He went to art school in San Francisco. And he teaches classes in Santa Fe. But he can't make a good living at it, so he drives around the countryside painting advertising signs on barns and other buildings. That's what he's doing here in Eldorado."

"Then he'll go back to Santa Fe from here?"

"Yes, but we may correspond. He's a very interesting man. I may get to know him better by letter than in person. Schoolteachers are restricted in their personal lives, you know."

"I don't understand," I said. "I thought when a woman worked she could become independent."

"Not teachers. The school board makes rules that try to keep a teacher under control. When you sign a contract you must agree to abide by the rules."

"What are the rules like? Like the ones you make for the scholars in your school?" I was sitting with my hands up in the air as we talked. Miss Katy had smeared them with a lemon-smelling unguent to bleach out the red.

"I must go to church every Sunday, and live under my father's roof. I can have a gentleman caller only one evening a week. I am never to step out alone with a gentleman who is not a member of my family."

She looked up from her fingernails and laughed. She said, "So this evening you're my chaperone, Maude. Think of that."

"I didn't know it was like that, Miss Katy. I thought teaching might be a way for a woman to be independent. There are not many respectable professions for a woman to follow to make her own way in the world."

"No, the world expects you to stay home and become a wife and mother. I like to teach, but I think of exchanging my many masters on the school board for the one master of a husband."

She then said, "So you've thought about teaching? You learn fast, Maude. You'd make a good teacher."

Miss Katy took the globe off the lamp and held the curling iron above the flame. When she wet her finger and touched it to the iron, the spit sizzled. "Now, it's hot enough. You do that, Maude. Heat the iron, test it, then while I hold this little paper around my hair, you roll a little curl right here. Count to five, then pull out the iron." I did as she instructed and made little curls that spilled down over her forehead.

As I worked, I continued our conversation. "Whatever I do, Miss Katy, I've got to earn enough to live on. I'm on my own with naught but what I gain by my own labor. Would teaching pay me enough?"

"Maybe if you taught in a city. But around here, you can't earn enough. If I didn't live at the ranch with my family, I couldn't manage. You see, a teacher gets paid by the month. For a beginning woman teacher, maybe thirty dollars a month. But if the school district only holds school for five months a year, then one hundred and fifty dollars is all the teacher gets. That's not enough to live on for twelve months out of the year."

The talk changed to Cody Collins. Of course, I'm very curious about him and opened the subject by telling

Miss Katy about the only conversation I ever had with him. You remember, Mama? In the store when I was so humiliated because I didn't have enough money to pay our bill and Mr. Collins offered to buy Daisy from me?

"That sounds like Cody. He's good-hearted," Miss Katy said. "He's my cousin. He's got the ranch our granddad started. When I was a little girl, Cody would tease me until I cried."

"People say that he is four-square," I said.

"Oh, yes. Quite responsible and upright, even if he does still tease me." For all our ease in talking, Miss Katy never expressed her opinion about me stepping out with her cousin, Cody Collins. What does she think, I wonder, about her cousin asking out someone as young as I am?

So, here I sit, Mama. I'll never be any more ready than I am right now. What will this evening bring?

Saturday, February 6, 1897

Mama, all I can say is it's a good thing we can't foretell the future. If we could, we'd have no moments of joy. Most of our lives, we would be cowering, waiting for certain calamity to strike.

As I wrote you last — and it was not so very long ago — I was excited about going to the Box Social. Now, I should be happily dreaming. Instead, I lay tossing and turning until I gave up on sleep. So, Mama, I'll tell you how it was.

The evening began like a fairy tale. Our Annie knocked on my door to tell me Mr. Collins was downstairs. Her eyes got big as saucers when she saw me all got up like I was. She circled me, still looking, then laughed aloud. I wish she could enjoy an evening out, too, but, of course, she can't — being Indian. But I knew she was happy I was going.

Downstairs in the parlor, Miss Katy was seated on the sofa with Mr. Jennings. Mrs. Steckler was by the stove warming herself. Mr. Collins stood in the middle of the room looking at the wax fruit. When I came in, Mr. Jennings jumped to his feet and both men stood at attention. Miss Katy had coached me so I knew what to do. I held out my hand to each in turn, just as cool as you please. You might say that they looked flabbergasted when they saw me.

Since you will be hearing more of Mr. Collins and Mr. Jennings, let me describe them. Mr. Jennings is a man almost my height. When I am wearing the dove-colored shoes with the little heels, I can look straight into his eyes, which are brown. His hair is thick, black, and curly. Even his mustache has little curls. He looks like he's comfortable in a suit even if he's not going to church or a funeral. His round face is open and ready to smile. His dress and manners separate him from the rough-and-ready men in Eldorado. Anyone who doubted his manliness, however, would be corrected on noticing his weatherbeaten visage and the muscles in his neck and shoulders, visible under the cloth of his coat.

Mr. Collins is opposite to Mr. Jennings in every way. In build, he's taller than I, and he's one long piece of gristle. His suit, boiled shirt, collar, and cravat did not sit comfortably on his body. Only his feet seemed at ease in his cowboy boots. Mr. Collins has nice regular features, but when his hat is off, I am drawn most to his blue eyes and the high forehead. Above his eyes, his brow is as white as any baby's in contrast to his sun-browned jaw and neck.

Mrs. Steckler took the most intense interest in my appearance. "Our dear Maude," she said. "Our ugly duckling has blossomed. Do you not think so, Mr. Collins?"

"Yes, ma'am," Mr. Collins said. "She looks mighty fine."

He seemed as uncomfortable with her attention as I

was. "Well, we better vamoose out of here," he said.

When he held my shawl for me — a good woolen one Lovey gave me — I could smell that Mr. Collins had put as much effort into getting ready as I had. Overall, there was a manlike aroma to him: the cedar smell of his woolen suit and the lingering smell of yellow soap. But there was a puzzling smell of roses, which I finally took to be from some tonic he had put on his hair. Altogether, he gave a very satisfying appearance even if he is thirty-four years old (which Miss Katy told me).

Miss Katy and Mr. Jennings walked ahead of us — for we walked to the Fire House. As you most likely remember, Mama, it is only about five hundred feet down the hill from the Palmer House. Mr. Collins and I walked side by side, not touching, not talking.

Finally, he cleared his throat and said, "The air's got a nice snap to it tonight, don't it, ma'am?"

While I tried to think what to answer, the silence stretched out and the stamping mill grew louder and louder like a big heartbeat. I said, "It's very nice." I said, "I'd be obliged if you didn't call me 'ma'am.' I'm too young to be a ma'am. Why don't you call me Maude?" As soon as I said it, I knew that by saying I was too young, I was also saying he was too old, but he didn't seem to catch that sense of it.

"How about 'Miss Maude'? Will that do?"

"All right," I said, although this still sounded very grown-up.

"I see they've moved the water wagon and the pumper outside the Fire House," I said, trying to keep up a conversation.

"Yes, and they've got the building well lighted.

There's been some polishing of lamp globes and reflectors for the Social tonight."

Since Mr. Collins was much my senior, and more experienced than I in social matters, I expected him to lead the way in conversation. Perhaps he was naturally silent and shy, but he seemed as nervous as I, often clearing his throat for several seconds before saying anything.

Inside, the building was ablaze with light. While our gentlemen took our wraps to a cloakroom on the far side of the large room, Miss Katy and I took our box suppers to the platform, unwrapped them, and put them on a table with others.

Once the box was out of my hands, I didn't know what to do with them. They hung at the end of my arms like red foreign growths. Since Miss Katy seemed at ease, I followed her example, holding my hands loosely clasped in front of me.

On the platform, the musicians got the fiddles and banjo out of the cases. There was a steady stream of people coming in the door — couples, some with children, and single men — bringing the cold outdoor air with them. The chairs around the sides of the room filled up, and people stood in the center of the room.

Lovey and Mr. Washburn came over, and Lovey was full of significant looks at me and Mr. Collins. "He's very handsome," she whispered to me. "You all make a nice couple. Maude, you need someone with a little height to look good with you." Mama, sometimes when Lovey finishes paying me a compliment, I feel like she's given me cold oatmeal.

126

I can say that Lovey and Mr. Washburn made a nice couple. Mr. Washburn stood very erect, even reared back a little, with his left arm held stiffly across his chest. Lovey held onto his left elbow with both hands like she was in danger of being blown away by a severe storm.

A caller on the platform persuaded the crowd to clear the floor, and sets were made up for square dancing. Mr. Collins and I were in the same set with Miss Katy and Mr. Jennings. The players started out with "Skip to My Lou," and I remembered it from when I was little. You were well, and you, Da, and I went to socials in the schoolhouse in Colorado, and Uncle Rab danced with me. But the next piece I didn't know, and I had to listen to the calls real close so I didn't get lost.

Concentrating on the music didn't take my mind off Mr. Collins, though. His hand, rough as mine, was warm and strong. When we do-sa-doed, he moved easy, like a willow in a breeze. In the promenade, his arm around my waist made me feel cherished and safe.

I'm afraid, Mama, that I was thinking sort of foolish and had wrapped myself in a world that only included Mr. Collins and me. For during the last dance before the break, I was rudely brought back to earth. With all my thoughts misted, I was going through the allemande left and realized I was holding onto the forearm of Flem and he was holding onto mine. You remember Flem? That viperous man from the incident in the dining room? I jerked back, but he gripped the tighter and pulled me close to his face. His breath stank of rotgut. "Save me a dance for later, sweetheart," he whispered. After we went into another figure, I watched to see what woman would be with that wretch. Flem's partner was another man. You'll remember that's not so unusual in a place like Eldorado where there are so few good women.

The cakewalk helped get my mind off Flem because Mr. Collins was by my side the whole time. He paid a dollar for us to enter. Set in each of the four corners of the room was a chair. On each chair was a layer cake. We partners shuffled around the edge of the room while the band played faster and faster until we were practically galloping. When the music stopped, the couple closest to each cake won it. I don't know why I'm writing all this to you, Mama. If you remember anything of your sojourn here on earth, you must remember about socials.

All that bouncing around heated up the room considerable. One of the firemen opened the big front door, but the people next to it yelled about the cold chill that came in. So, I fanned myself with my hand and restrained myself from declaring how sweaty I was. Mr. Collins produced a big white handkerchief and mopped his face with it. I did pity the men in those wool suits and high collars.

The square dance caller pulled the table stacked with box suppers to the center of the platform and put on an auctioneer's voice for the box auction. This time he had no trouble getting the attention of the gathering. Everyone crowded around the platform. Even the men without women partners, those who had been standing near the door and going outside from time to time — to have a nip from their bottles to judge from their behavior — edged closer to the front.

The caller talked up the crowd, picking up a box and

smelling it, then declaring what delights it held for the lucky bidder.

"Chitlins," he said. "I just know it's chitlins. And who but a Southern belle would be putting chitlins in a box? There must be a Johnny Reb in this crowd who'd appreciate some real Southern cooking. What am I bid for this lovely box?"

The bidding usually started at fifteen or twenty cents and got very spirited as some crafty old miner ran the bid up on a young man determined to share the box supper with his sweetheart.

The first box up, however, turned out to belong to a little girl, maybe seven years old. Her face was a mix of delight and dismay when her box went for $1.75, but the winning bidder was an old miner — straight from his digs, still wearing his overalls, boots, and hat. He was just set on getting himself some home-cooked food.

Because Lovey is still a bride, everyone laughed when Mr. Macbride, her husband's boss, ran the bidding up on Mr. Washburn. Mr. Washburn finally ended up paying five dollars for the company of his own wife to share food that came out of his own kitchen.

I was getting nervous about what to do when my box came up. What kind of encouragement should I give Mr. Collins so he'd know it was my box? I hoped Miss Katy's box would come up first so I could follow her example. However, mine came up before hers. I needn't have worried about giving Mr. Collins a clue. He must have been watching my face because he grinned at me right away. I nodded to him, and he started the bidding at one dollar. Maybe he thought he'd walk away with the box for that, but no.

From the back of the crowd came a man's voice. There was no mincing around with a fifteen-cent raise. The bid went right to five dollars. Mr. Collins swiveled around to see who was bidding against him. The auctioneer started up his chant, "Whaddo I hear?" I was getting nervous that Mr. Collins wouldn't get my box because I knew who bid so much, even though I couldn't see him.

While Mr. Collins was still intent on spying out the man who bid, the auctioneer brought down his hammer and sold my box lunch to Flem.

Now that degenerate was easy to see, going up to the auctioneer waving a five-dollar bill over his head. With my box clutched under his arm, he came through the crowd toward me. People parted way, everyone watching to see what would happen. I was so miserable I could have retched.

Mr. Collins's face was beet-red all the way past his forehead. Alongside his left eye a vein popped up and wriggled like a worm. He stepped in front of me. Looking over his shoulder I could not see any hesitation on Flem's face.

"I get to collect the girl that goes with this box," he said.

"Hey, Cody, fair's fair. You weren't fast enough," yelled a man's voice.

"Steady there, ole hoss, no use getting riled," said another.

"Cody, perhaps . . ." I heard Mr. Jennings start to say.

Mr. Collins wasn't hearing anything. He grabbed Flem's right arm and twisted it behind him and shoved him toward the door. Flem was as tall as Mr. Collins and heavier, but the strong drink that gave him courage might also have unbalanced him.

The men in the crowd surged to the door, following the two outside. On the stage, the auctioneer grabbed another box and tried to get the bidding started.

Miss Katy came over and put her arm around me. Tears were just about to spill from my eyes, but I determined to hold them back.

"Why do men have to act like that?" I asked Miss Katy. "We were having such fun. Why does that blackguard Flem force his attentions on me?"

"I suspect hard drinking leaves him without a lick of sense. I wish Cody hadn't taken him outside, though. I'm afraid of what might happen. Cody was awful mad."

"I'm pulled this way and that. I'm worried about Mr. Collins, but I'm mad, too. I feel like a bone that two dogs are fighting over. Why is it, Miss Katy, when you've not done anything wrong that men can say or do something that makes you feel dirty?"

"I don't know, my dear. I suppose that's why we need a male to protect us from the kind of men whose words or actions make us feel shame for being the weaker sex."

Soon, I knew that such a male wanted to protect me. Mr. Collins came back into the Fire House holding aloft my frazzled box like a trophy. In his shirtsleeves, his collar loose and standing up and his hair hanging down on his brow, he looked like the shining victor.

Without pausing, he thrust the box into my hands and went toward the platform. The auctioneer took a step backward as Cody Collins thrust something at him. It turned out to be a ten-dollar bill. In a voice loud enough that everyone could hear, he said, "Here's the highest bid fair and square." In a more rasping voice, he said, "I'd hate to think that anyone running a box auction would be so low-down as to take a bribe to close out a bid early."

"No, no, Cody. Of course not," the auctioneer said, but you could see how scared he was.

Well, Mama, that put the stopper on the fun for the night. On our walk home, Mr. Jennings and I remained silent. Taking advantage of being a cousin, Miss Katy took Mr. Collins to task for being so fast with his fists and slow with his brain. The shine started to go out of him.

"Aw, Katy," he said, "there was no way I could have won out on that auction. Flem could have forced me way high without ever having to put up anything himself or he could bribe the auctioneer, which is what I think he did."

"Well, no damage would have been done if he'd eaten the box supper with Maude. They would have been in plain sight of everyone in the building," Miss Katy said.

"So would I have been in plain sight," he retorted. "I'd be standing there looking like a fool in front of everyone."

So, you see, Mama, how troublesome it is. Maybe I do need a male protector like Miss Katy says. But was Mr. Collins protecting me? Or was he protecting his own honor?

And no matter what Mr. Collins did this evening, he can't be at my side always. I fear this scum, Flem. I'm afraid I have not heard the last of him.

Saturday, February 13, 1897

The days since the Social have been cold and windy. It's been a good time to be indoors. I've no time to be mooning around, though. I've taken on the education of Annie.

Mama, I hope you are hovering around here in the afternoons so you can see her. And hear her. I was right in thinking Annie could talk. Ever since that day she took me to the Centennial Bar, I've been coaxing her into talking more and more. It used to be that after we cleaned up from dinner, Annie would disappear. Once or twice I saw her going into the shed out back — for what reason, I don't know. But now, we have class in my room. I'm teaching Annie to read and write. She talks to me in a low voice that is rusty from lack of use.

The only books I have are the Bible and your old set of Shakespeare plays, so I write sentences and words in a tablet and get her to read them and copy them. I draw little pictures as I remember them from my first reader. Do you recall it, Mama? I write sentences like:

> Nightingales sing in time of spring.
> A dog will bite a thief at night.
> An eagle's flight is out of sight.

Annie knows all the letters and has got the idea of reading. I think, though, all these years of silence under Mrs. Steckler's roof have dimmed her mind somewhat. She looks at me often, fearful of making a mistake.

Some ideas, even simple ideas, she doesn't know. Like "sisters." I drew a picture of two girls in black skirts and white waists — a short girl with a long black braid and a tall one with a curly mop of hair. Underneath I wrote "All Eve's daughters are Sisters under their Skins."

She asked, "You and me?"

"Yes," I said.

"Friends? Sister means friend?"

Mama, my heart ached for her. She has no memory of a family at all. She was certainly never deceived into thinking she was part of the Steckler family. Even though she is older than I, she is very childlike. If I say a word in any way critical, her face closes up and shuts me out.

Today I drew for her a picture of me and Mr. Collins at the Social that showed us dancing. Annie held her hand over her mouth and giggled.

I was feeling much elated because a cowboy from the Tic-Tac-Toe brought a note from Mr. Collins asking could he call on me Monday, February 22. With Mrs. Steckler's permission, I agreed to the day. If the weather turns good, we can take a walk. Even as I taught Annie, I kept remembering the warmth of Mr. Collins's arm around me. On the tablet, I wrote for Annie to copy, "Mrs. Cody Collins."

Although she holds a needle nicely and stitches very

well, Annie grasps a pencil and pushes on it like she was scribing in granite. While she concentrated over the script, there was a tap on the door and it swung open. Lovey came in. I grabbed the tablet and pushed it into Annie's lap.

"What are you doing?" Lovey asked. She seemed surprised to see Annie sitting at my table.

"Annie is learning to read and write," I said.

"What a waste of time, Maude. If she was bright, she would have learned a long time ago." Lovey spoke as though Annie couldn't understand her. Annie responded by pretending not to hear. It didn't seem to occur to Lovey that Annie had never had a day of schooling in her life.

Lovey threw her shawl on the bed and stood in the square of warm sunlight from the window. Then she pulled a little book from her pocket and handed it to me. Such a pretty little thing it was, having pressed cardboard covers in maroon with gold-embossed designs of every description. There was a dove trailing ribbons, a sailing ship, an animal with long teeth, the man in the moon and stars, and such a variety of other patterns. Pasted on the cover was an oval drawing of a woman holding a Japanese fan in front of her face in a coy way. The word "Mikado" was printed on the cover in very fancy letters. Lovey didn't know what it meant, nor did I.

Along the spine ran the word "Album." Lovey said Mr. Washburn bought it for her in El Paso, and it was her memory book. Girls at school used to have them, but nothing as handsome as this one.

"May I read what's in it?" I asked.

"Lordy, yes. There's not much personal there. I brought it so you could write in it."

What could I write? I thought of all the silly verses school kids wrote. Lovey and I leafed through it together.

On the first page there was a drawing in color of three women in Japanese costumes. It was a puzzle because they had English faces. Lovey had written on this page:

> *In this book*
> *With its pages so fair*
> *I wish all my friends*
> *to write.*

There were three verses with sentiments about violets and roses; there were four (all from males) with this verse:

> *When you see a cat run up a tree*
> *Pull his tail and think of me.*

There were somber verses, and sentimental ones, and moral ones. On a blank page I wrote:

> *Not like the rose may our friendship wither,*
> *But like the evergreen live forever.*
> *Maude Oakley Brannigan*

I drew roses in the top corners of the page, fir trees below, and connected them with a turning, weaving ribbon.

"Oh, Maude Oakley Brannigan, I'm going to miss you even if you are daft," Lovey said. Her face was very mournful.

"What do you mean?" I asked. "How can you miss me when I'm right here?"

"Well, I won't be here. Mr. Washburn and I are moving to Denver."

"Denver? Whatever for?" I asked.

"The regional office for the company is there. They're going to shut down here in Eldorado. Mr. Washburn wants to stay with the company, so he'll have to go where they send him. In a few years he can work his way up to a better job."

"Don't you want to go?"

"Oh, sure," she said. "We'll have a better house and all. But Denver's so big compared with here."

"I suppose everyone will be leaving. What will I do if your mother closes down the Palmer House?"

"You certainly don't have anything to worry about. Cody Collins can make a good living from ranching even if Eldorado disappears from the face of the earth."

"What does that have to do with me?" I asked. I didn't know how I felt about Mr. Collins, and I was getting tired of people trying to push me at him.

"Maw says he wants to see you again. It's because he's got his hat set for you. Didn't you enjoy his company at the Social?"

"Yes. What I had of it, before he went tearing into a fight like a mad bull. But it's hard getting acquainted with both of us being shy."

"You're going to marry him, I know, and have plenty of time to get acquainted after that."

"Sure," I said, "marry in haste, repent in leisure."

After Lovey left, Mama, I did begin to think that I've got a dilemma. Here I am trying to get away from Eldorado. But what if Eldorado just up and closes down while I'm still getting ready to go? Will I have a choice about my life? Will I have to marry Mr. Collins because there's no other place to turn?

Sunday, February 21, 1897

Mama, I give thanks once again that I've got a sturdy body and I'm glad something or somebody (you, Mama?) gives me the strength to act even when I'm sore afraid.

Last night tested my courage to its very limits. When I went to sleep, I could hear the usual Saturday night noises: the hubbub coming from the Centennial Bar, horse hooves striking the frozen street, men's voices arguing, doors slamming.

When I awoke, the noise was nearer, right out in the hall. At first I thought someone was trying to batter down my door. Just as I realized the blows were on Annie's door, I heard the splinter of wood and a crash as her door gave way.

I huddled in my bed under the covers rigid and shivering. A terrible banging came from Annie's room. There was no one on this second floor except Annie and me. Even if her life was threatened, she wouldn't scream. I was the only one who knew that she needed help.

Another crash. My room was dark as pitch. With shaky fingers I lighted my lamp. Because my room was so cold, I had gone to bed fully clothed except for shoes. I didn't think about putting them on.

I cast my mind about for a weapon. At that time I never thought about my knife, which is always with me. I guess I don't think of it as a weapon. It would probably not have done me much good anyway. They say women don't know how to use a knife properly. There was nothing else at hand, not even a poker.

Quietly, I slipped the bolt on my door and opened it a thin crack. Something slammed in Annie's room. I threw back my door and stepped across the hall. Annie's door hung open.

At first, all I could make out was the figure of a man. I saw his back, a fist pulled up, shoulder muscles balled. Annie's bed had crashed. The slats lay scattered on the floor.

The man turned, and I saw it was Flem. Beyond him, slumped against the wall, was Annie. Her wide eyes stared across the arms she held up to protect her head. Her white shirtwaist was torn.

His eyes rolled greasily, like some dumb brute's. "You," he said to me, "you damned bitch." He started toward me, and I knew he had made a mistake. It was not Annie's room he wanted but mine.

For just an instant, for less time than it takes to tell, I felt dirty and shamed by him. Now that I think about that moment, I think that's how women feel when they just stand and let men brutalize them and violate them. But the feeling was soon replaced by a surge of rage, of Da's black Irish temper.

Flem wasn't used to being attacked by a woman, I

guess. He looked pretty surprised when I rushed at him and flung the lamp in his face. Going low under his thrashing arms, I grabbed a slat. Keeping low, and guided by his curses, I whacked him right across the knees with the slat. He fell into the mess that had been the bed.

By the time he got to his feet I had got in back of him, intending to drive him from the room or kill him. I hit him higher in the back and felt the board splinter in my hands. I dropped to my hands and knees and felt out another slat. Then I crawled to the door. I could hear Flem's arms flailing the air above me.

Out the door I went, mostly by feel. I rose to my feet in the hall. By the blast of cold air coming in, I knew the outside door to the steps was open. I roared as loud as I could, so Flem would know where I was. Then I slammed the door to my room.

Flem hurtled out of Annie's room into the hall. As for seeing him, I couldn't. He was just a black mass in total darkness. But he reeked with coal oil from the lamp, so I gauged by my nose when he was in the right spot.

Like a Greek battering at the gates of Troy, I gripped my slat lengthwise and ran at him. What a noise he made going down those steep steps. A long silence followed. It's probably sinful to say, or even think, but I hoped he had broken his neck in that fall. I was still boiling with hate and rage.

Someone came around the first-floor porch with a lantern. "Maude," I heard Mrs. Steckler bellow, "what's going on up there? What's all that racket?"

By the lantern light, I saw Flem pull himself up, holding onto the railing. "My Lord," I heard Mrs. Steckler say. Flem seemed to say something to her. Then he was gone into the night.

A man's voice, slurred, yelled from the street, "Hey, Flem, did you get what you went for?" There was a whinny-laugh.

"Mrs. Steckler," I yelled, "would you bring the lantern up, please? I think Annie's hurt."

When Mrs. Steckler threw the light into Annie's room, she gasped and said, "My stars. I hope I m'y die."

From the door clear to the broken window, everything in that room was total destruction. Glass from my broken lamp glittered on the floor. The air was drenched with the smell of coal oil. Covers and bed railings were scattered. Against the wall lay a muddle of black and white. Never a sound came from there. Never a sound did Annie make. Disregarding the broken glass under my bare feet, I flew to her. Her white blouse was shredded and bloody. Strands of black hair mingled with the blood that seeped from her nose and mouth.

I cradled her head in my lap and talked soft to her. Poor innocent victim. This was supposed to have been my fate. Or maybe Flem had even worse in mind.

Finally, her eyes opened. Terror, blind terror, filled them. She turned her head as though to flinch away from another blow. Maybe, just then, she expected brutality from every pair of round eyes that got close to her.

"My Lord, my Lord, look at this room," Mrs. Steckler said. "Maude, can you get her to your room? It's freezing cold in here. I'll go get water and linen."

The lamp in Annie's room was, by some miracle, un-broken. I lighted it. I half carried, half dragged Annie to my room and put her into my bed. Using cold water from my jug, I made a towel compress to put on her face.

After a long while, Mrs. Steckler came back with the big kettle. I knew she had had to build up the fire and wait for the water to heat. We undressed Annie to her undergarments and Mrs. Steckler examined her for bro-ken bones. There was a lump as big as a hen's egg on the back of her head. Mrs. Steckler looked in her eyes and said she didn't have a concussion of the brain.

As you remember, Mama, Dr. Rudd left Eldorado two years ago before you got so sick. The army won't let their military doctor leave the post, so patients have to go to him. When I suggested we should take Annie to the doctor at the post, Mrs. Steckler just snorted.

When we had done what we could for Annie, Mrs. Steckler looked at my feet. "Good Lord, Maude. Stop bleeding all over the rugs. Can't you do something about your feet?" The soles of my bare feet were crisscrossed with cuts. I poured clean water in the basin and, sitting in the one chair in the room, put both feet in the water.

While I brushed my feet gingerly to locate the glass, Mrs. Steckler stood in the middle of the room with arms akimbo. Her hair was wound up in rag curls, and her face was shiny pink. She appeared to be casting about in her mind to find in this situation a grievance to herself much bigger than the terror that was visited on Annie and me.

She started off rumbling and built up steam as she

went. "What's the meaning of all this, Maude? What was that man doing up here? Who do you think will pay for the damage to Our Annie's room?"

When she took breath, I protested. "It was not our doing, ma'am. That blackguard came up here and busted into Annie's room thinking it was mine. It was me he wanted to get back at."

"If you ask me, the both of you are in on it. One of you asked him up here, I know. Trying to turn my house into a bawdyhouse. Tell me this, who unbarred the door at the top of the stairs? And why are both of you fully dressed if you weren't expecting company?"

My rage at Flem had drained off while I tended Annie, but I felt my gorge rising again. "I don't know how he got through the outside door. If he'd been invited, he wouldn't have to break down Annie's door, would he? As for having our clothes on, I don't know about Annie, but I sleep with mine on because it's too cold in this room to do without." I spoke pertly, but was afraid to say any further for fear of losing my job.

So that's how it stood until this morning. I brought Annie's bedclothes and mattress to my room and slept the night with a slat by my side.

This morning Mrs. Steckler was in the kitchen when Annie and I came in. The fire was just catching good and roared in the chimney. Yee hadn't yet arrived.

Annie wouldn't stay in bed. Her walk was slow and stiff. Her arms were bruised from taking the blows aimed at her head. Her left ear was swollen and shiny purple. A puffed upper lip and swollen cheek were the other visible signs of the brutality poor Annie suffered.

144

Worse than these were her eyes. She wouldn't look at me or talk to me. When I tried to help her get dressed, she slid past me into her room. I wonder if Annie feels all the time the dirtiness and self-disgust from being an Indian woman that I am made to feel only occasionally for being a woman.

I walked like a cripple, too, with the bottoms of my feet burning from the stockings touching them. We must have been a sorry-looking pair.

Mrs. Steckler's hair was as frizzy, her face as powdered, and her waist as small as ever. Her bearing was very upright. "I can see, after the unfortunate happening last night, that I have been too lenient with you two. As hard as I have tried, I have failed to instill Christian morality into your character. You two have been sneaking out at night. While I slept you've been roving like harlots."

I interrupted, "Ma'am, that is not true."

Mrs. Steckler bellowed, "Maude, how dare you talk back to me? Have you learned nothing of decent living while you have been under my roof?"

She continued, "I might have expected this from Our Annie. Being Indian, and Apache at that. Everyone knows about the base nature of their women. I must keep her animal nature under control. Henceforth, Our Annie will be chained to her bed every night."

"But she did nothing," I said. Mama, I was so angry. Mrs. Steckler stood there like she was measuring me up, waiting to hear how much I dared to say.

"Maude, I should let you go," Mrs. Steckler said and paused, as though waiting for me to protest further and

145

thus give her the excuse. I remained quiet. I thought, chains for me, too. By being mute, I'm consenting to be chained to my bed.

She had something else on her mind. She sighed. "But, wayward as you are, you're still young. My Christian conscience . . ." Then, more briskly, she said, "There's not enough work around here to keep you occupied. The Devil finds work for idle hands. From now on, you will clean the Methodist Church, all of it, including the Men's Reading Room, two times a week. Let's see. You can clean Monday after Sunday's service and Thursday after the Wednesday night prayer meeting. Maybe the church atmosphere will have a beneficial effect."

If I hadn't been so mad, I could have laughed. Mama, this woman seems to think that time spent in the church on my knees scrubbing the floor is the same as time spent in the church praying. It's also curious, I thought, that she sends Annie to clean the bar and me to clean the church. It's like she's paying tithes in two worlds.

Well, Mama, more work won't hurt me. I've still got my job and a place to stay.

Today at the dinner table, the men looked at me different, like they knew the true story of how Flem got the bejabbers knocked out him. Just a little amused they were, and quite respectful.

But poor Annie. I found enough extra slats in the toolshed to set her bed up in my room. Mrs. Steckler had the window and door to Annie's room boarded up. Annie is suffering, I know. Maybe, with time, we can gain back lost ground.

Thursday night, February 25, 1897

Mama, I've been so busy, I've scarce found time to think. Since Sunday, Mrs. Steckler has been stern and distant, but has held her tongue. She's found much more work for me to do — like turning out and airing the downstairs guest rooms even though most have been empty all the time I've been here.

Monday, Mr. Collins came to the Palmer House for dinner. While I washed up afterward, he waited for me in the parlor. Mrs. Steckler joined him there. Not knowing what she might tell him of Saturday night's happenings, I wanted to talk with him alone so I could tell him the truth.

When I came out from the kitchen I had on my coat. We walked out to the town corrals. Mr. Collins was dressed in his work clothes: leather chaps, well-worn boots, and a sweat-stained hat with the brim mangled into a peak at the front. He had just today brought one bunch of cattle into town and still had to collect more from another canyon. As we walked around the outside of the corral, Mr. Collins checked to make sure there were no openings in the juniper-post fence. Even though he was more at ease in these clothes and this activity than he was at the Box Social, he still seemed shy.

He listened without a word as I told him about Flem. Because he didn't say anything or look at me, I didn't know how he was taking it.

At length, he said, "I'm going to marry you, Miss Maude, and it looks like the sooner the better. As long as you're working in a public house in a mining camp like Eldorado, you're going to attract snakes like Flem."

Well, Mama, I can't tell you how surprised I was. I thought a man was supposed to ask you to marry him, not just declare that's the way it's going to be. I'm not sure I like this way of doing things.

"We don't know each other yet," I protested.

Mr. Collins leaned his arms on top of the wired-to-gether posts and gazed across an acre of dusty, bawling cattle. I guess he had been giving the marriage idea some thought because he said, "You know, some men marry mail-order brides. Women who come from the East or all the way from Sweden or someplace. Sight unseen. At least, I've seen you and I'm satisfied with the way you look." He grinned at me out of his dusty face like he had paid me a big compliment.

This was pretty weak stuff compared with Shakespeare. "One fairer than my love! The all-seeing sun ne'er saw her match since first the world begun." Mr. Collins sure couldn't hold a candle to Romeo.

My face must have reflected some of what I was feeling, for Mr. Collins said, "I'm no great shakes as a fancy talker. But when you marry me, you'll not want. We'll always have plenty of beef to eat." He enjoyed his joke, stretching his grin toward his right ear. What fine lines he had in his face. I could feel my fingers carving them in wood.

He continued, "You'll like the ranch. I've been living in a line shack on the headwaters of the Sapello, but I'll build you a real house. It's real pretty up there. Clean. Not like this mining camp."

Well, there it is. I'd like to say it is my first proposal of marriage, but it's more like a command. I told Mr. Collins I had to think about it, and I do, for it's apparent that Eldorado is going downhill. I have to take some action for my future.

As soon as Mr. Collins gets his cattle gathered up, he and his crew will drive them to the railroad at Santa Cecilia, take them on the train to Arizona, and deliver them to the Indian reservation. Mr. Collins said I should have my answer ready for when he returns.

Not a word of love passed between us. But, I must remember, Romeo didn't promise to keep beef on the table, either. Maybe it's just my youth that makes me yearn for tender feelings.

*

Just when I've considered matters in a cool light and think I can make a mature decision such as Lovey and Mrs. Steckler urge on me, something else happens which makes me wonder if I can subdue my nature and find happiness living the life that most women live.

You see, Mama, the work Mrs. Steckler set me to as a punishment has opened up a whole new world to me. This morning, I went to Reverend Robinson's house, he being the same who buried you. He walked across the street and opened the church for me and my mop and bucket.

Of course, I've been there regular on Sundays since I started at the Palmer House, but it's different in non-church times. More dust than holiness fills the air. As he showed me around, Reverend Robinson pointed out what I should do. Then he commended Mrs. Steckler for being such a fine Christian woman to send me to clean.

Right inside the entrance, the preacher pushed open a door to a room I've never been in. The Men's Reading Room. A small room, but with good light from the high window and lamps so working men can study or read there in the evening. As soon as Reverend Robinson left, I hurried through the cleaning. I wanted time to examine the contents of that room.

Mama, what a good idea this is. There should also be a reading room for women and children. I hear men at the Palmer House laugh at women for their shallow views on life, yet how can women form opinions when there is so little information at hand for their education?

There were two glass-fronted bookcases with a whole set of Shakespeare's plays, books about our Founding Fathers, Franklin and Jefferson and many others, books by J. S. Mill, Aristotle, Thackeray. I can't name them all. Stacked in bins were magazines the like of which I've never seen before. The *Atlantic Monthly*, I remember, and *The Century*. In *The Century*, a story about the great artist John Sargent and his painting. There was also a sketch of a woman (yes! a woman!) painting. Such a wealth of material she had. A folding stool with a pocket to store things, brushes of all kinds, a box with colors.

Then I was folding a newspaper, an old copy of the *New York Times*, to put it away. My eye was caught by a headline of something I'd been told many times did not exist.

AMERICAN ART ASSOCIATION SALE

Miss Cassatt's Work — John Sargent
and His Decorations Arrive in Boston

I scanned until I saw the name Cassatt again. I memorized what it said.

Mary Cassatt's pictures at the Durand-Ruel Galleries should on no account be missed. It is not too much to say that she is today the strongest and most personal of American women painters.

How excited I was, Mama. There are women artists. There are American women artists. There is one American woman painter so remarkable that the *New York Times* says her work "should on no account be missed."

What a blessing it is to know that there are other females in the world whose fingers itch to paint, to carve, to create. At least one woman did it — did what her nature drove her to do. She did it so well that her work is compared with men's.

My head was so full of these Jubilee words that I almost didn't hear the noon whistle calling me back to the Palmer House.

Monday, March 1, 1897

Mama, I have brought calamity on my head. This time, I can clearly see that I'm no victim. I am at fault. I hope your spirit is still with me in this house of ill repute where I find myself. When last I wrote, I thought I had two choices for my future: marriage to Mr. Collins or an artist's life. Now I'm not sure that my future holds anything but shame.

Two circumstances combined to make me tempt fate. The first is my anger at the unjustness which Mrs. Steckler imposes on Annie and me. Every night at eight o'clock, Mrs. Steckler comes upstairs with her lantern. With her face set in pious lines, she chains Annie to her bed. On Annie's ankle she puts a leather manacle with a hasp, the kind they might use to restrain a madman. A thin chain hooked to the hasp loops around the ironwork railing at the foot of the bed and is fastened with a lock. In the morning Mrs. Steckler comes and unlocks her.

I could cut through the leather strap with the knife I carry and told Annie so. She doesn't look at me or respond in any way. Neither does she pay any attention to Mrs. Steckler. Our landlady might as well be chaining a stump to the bed.

As for me, Mrs. Steckler finds excuses to impose her will at every turn. On Saturday it rained, then turned very cold during the night. When I came out Sunday morning to go to church everything sparkled clear and my spirits lifted. Big boys and little alike were on the slope by the Fire House, sledding and sliding down the frozen road. In the street in front of the Palmer House, water lay in frozen strips in the wagon ruts. On impulse, I took a little run and skated down the street on a long stretch of ice. I was a child again, just enjoying the sensation of being. It was only for a moment, for I heard Mrs. Steckler bellowing from the porch, "Maude, what do you think you're doing?"

Since she had to get to church herself, she hadn't much time for her sermon to me, but she did make me stay home to help Yee in the kitchen.

Harboring in the back of my mind my resentment at her harsh treatment, but also thinking of more pleasant recent events, I began to dwell on the newspaper story about Mary Cassatt. Many of her subjects were women and children. If I am to be a woman artist, I do need to practice on real people. Annie won't look at me, much less sit for me. Lovey has already left town. Miss Katy is either teaching or out at the ranch. I thought of Venus Adonna. She had already said she would pose. But where? I couldn't go to Peacock Gulch. It was too cold to be sitting still outdoors. My room was the only place.

When this idea came to me, I didn't think, "I'll do this to get back at Mrs. Steckler," but I did think to deceive her by asking Venus to come to my room after Sunday dinner when Mrs. Steckler always took a long nap.

So I gave the message to Yee, and by some method that I haven't yet fathomed, he got the message to Venus.

At the appointed hour she came on foot and I whisked her upstairs to my room. I had my paper and crayons ready, but it took me some time to get her seated so that the light was just right on her. She was dressed quite soberly in a walking skirt and jacket. Looking at herself in the wavery mirror, she removed the jacket, loosened her shirtwaist at the neck and wrists, and pulled loose some tresses to hang in front of her ears. She is very beautiful and seems to practice an art in making herself more so.

Annie was in the room, sitting on the bed. Venus looked at her curiously. As I gave her history, I reflected that Venus might know more about her than I do.

When I told about Flem, Venus said, "I heard about that. Flem is a bad customer. You watch out. His cronies razzed him because they know you got the best of him."

"Do you think Continental will buy out Flem's claim like some people say?" I asked. I had started my sketch as we talked. Venus knew how to sit perfectly still yet look relaxed.

"They already did, I heard. He's spent most of his money already on booze and women. It wasn't such a big strike as he said, though."

"I just wish he'd leave here — go away."

"He will. This place is closing down. It's time for me to be moving on, too."

"Do you have enough saved yet?" I asked.

"Just about. One of my regulars is coming this week — a gentleman from the Solomon's Mines main office in San Francisco. He's always very generous."

"Have you decided on a stage name?"

"No," she said. "I need more ideas. What's your middle name, Maude?"

"Oakley. Maude Oakley Brannigan," I told her.

Quietly, we laughed at the idea that any of my solid names would fit Venus. The whole building was quiet except for the wind rippling the sheet-metal roof.

The door was not bolted since I didn't think there was any danger of discovery. When it crashed open, I spun around, ready to do battle with Flem again. But Mrs. Steckler stood in the door. She looked as black as thunder.

"Maude, you've gone too far, bringing this harlot into my house," she bellowed.

Mrs. Steckler stood aside from the door and pointed downstairs. "Birds of a feather flock together," she said. "Maude, if I had any doubts about your character, they've been removed. You are fired. You and your friend get out of my house right now."

What could I say, Mama? I had willfully and wrongfully brought this wrath on my head, and I knew it.

Venus, just as cool as you please, pulled on her jacket, fixed her hair, and swept past Mrs. Steckler as though that lady were a bad-smelling pile of manure.

I, more flustered, started to gather up my things. "Just go," she bellowed. "Get out of my sight."

So I clutched the box in which I keep these tablets, these that are my writing to you, Mama, and left. Without a coat or a shawl, I felt like a character of a novel by Mrs. Stowe.

Venus was waiting for me in the street. "What a

155

bitch," she said. "You're better off out of her place. Why didn't you give her a piece of your mind?"

"It was my fault," I said. "I shouldn't have given her reason."

"You mean me?" Venus asked. A frown made two creases between her eyes.

"It's not your fault, Venus," I said. The cold wind raised goose bumps on my arms. "What am I to do? I've got no place to go. I suppose I can go back to the soddy."

"She called me a harlot. I ought to go back in there and give her something to think about," Venus said.

"No, Venus. Don't lose your temper like last time."

"I did, didn't I? But I'd had a little wine on that occasion."

"I've got to get out of this cold," I said, stomping my feet and beating my arms against my sides. I started down the street in the direction of our old soddy.

Venus trotted alongside trying to understand where I hoped to find shelter.

"Come on, Maude. You can't stay there. You'll freeze to death. Come on with me to Peacock Gulch. Miss Peggy won't mind. We've got two rooms no one is using. The girls are clearing out because business is so bad."

I stood stock-still. Me in Peacock Gulch! My reputation would be ruined forever.

A blast of wind blew snow in my face. In my room at the Palmer House I slept in my clothes under a blanket and quilt. At the soddy, I had no bedding, no fire, no real door to close. And Flem to worry about. If I didn't freeze to death, he would probably kill me. Venus was right.

To survive — just for one night — I had to give up worrying about what people would think. It would do me no good to protect my good name and be dead.

I said, "I'm not meaning to insult you, Venus, but I must say this. I have no place to go, and I do thank you for your offer of hospitality. I will go with you. But I will not traffic in your kind of trade."

As to my other worry that I might catch a horrible disease there, I kept that to myself. I had no wish to hear Venus deride me again for my fears.

"You won't be bothered, Maude. There's a bolt on the inside of the door. You can open it or not, as you choose. I'll see if I can't get your things sent over from the Palmer House."

So, here I am, Mama. I've sunk almost to the lowest level a woman can fall. At least I don't work here. But what if there is no other way open to me to earn my living?

When Venus brought me into the kitchen here, Miss Peggy and the two other soiled doves who work here were present. Yee's wife was there, too, but people act like she isn't. The women are kind and call me poor little lamb. But you can tell they are coarse women. One wears the same vanilla-smelling perfume as Mrs. Steckler. Even though it's afternoon, they still wear wrappers which flap open so that I see large milk-white thighs with blue veins. One of them is always puffing on a little brown cigar.

I'm in a room by myself now — a bedroom. Nice,

157

except that it has too much furniture and too much red. Someplace in the house, a piano is being played. Before dusk, looking across the gulch at the steep slope on the other side, I saw small shacks with open windows facing this way. Cribs, Venus said they were called. She said in the summers when Eldorado was booming each crib had a woman who leaned out the window and tried to entice a man customer to come up the steep trail.

Vulgar, Venus said they were. The lowest of the fallen women. So, you see, Mama, even here, in the direst straits, I continue to learn. Now I know that some doves are more soiled than others.

I hope Cody Collins gets back soon. Though why I say that, I don't know. He is likely not to believe in my innocence nor want to marry a woman who lives in a house of ill repute.

Mama, I'm glad you did not live to see this day of my shame. What shall I do?

Tuesday, March 2, 1897

Mama, I'm still in this house of ill repute in Peacock Gulch. But it's not doing its usual business. It's more like a hospital now. Several injured men from the Fire Company have been brought here. The soiled doves have become angels of mercy. I've been tearing snowy bed linen into strips while I watch over my own patient.

Last night, I was sitting in this same red upholstered chair, unable to sleep, straining to hear every voice, fearful that every footstep might stop in front of-the door to this room, that the doorknob might turn.

In the midst of my dreadful imaginings, I got the most awful feeling, like the world was holding its breath. It took me an instant to realize that the stamping mill had stopped. It was just like breathing. You do it all the time without thinking about it. Then if it stops . . . Well, this scared me even more than my thoughts had.

Doors slammed, and I could hear people running outside. Yee had sent my trunk from the Palmer House, so I had my shawl to throw about my head and shoulders. I joined the crowd. There are bawdyhouses all up and down Peacock Gulch, and their inhabitants were in the street in every kind of dress and undress. In the quiet street, they stood and muttered, full of wonder.

Not wanting to be seen in this company, I started rapidly down the road toward Main Street. At the exact same instant that I saw light flare up from downtown, I heard the fire bell ring.

Fire! As you know, Mama, with all the wooden buildings, not much water to damp down the flames, and the wind blowing, fire is the biggest menace to a mining camp.

The Gulch road filled with people running. "Fellows, take buckets with you," I heard a woman yell. "It's the Mill," someone said. "No, it's on Main Street."

The last voice was right beside me. I recognized it to be Flem's. In my haste, I had let the shawl slip from my head. When I turned to locate him, I was looking right into his eyes. By this time, all of us running people had reached the end of Peacock Gulch where it meets Main Street. From pure fright of Flem, I leaped out ahead of the crowd.

Pounding toward me were two apparitions which sight I hope never to see again. Two horses, whinnying in pain, galloped down the middle of the street. Fire streamed from their manes and tails.

I felt Flem grab at my shoulder, and for a fraction of a second, I turned to fight loose. All his attention was on me. As I wrenched free of Flem's grasp, I threw myself off the street and down the embankment.

This morning, Flem's body was found in that same arroyo only a few yards from where I had landed. From the looks of things, it was said, Flem and one of the horses met head-on. His chest was caved in. I'm afraid he went to meet his Maker with murder in his heart.

By the time I crawled to the road, most of the crowd

160

had passed by. As I came abreast of the Fire House, I could see that the fire was most fierce at the stables. As I got closer, I saw the firemen working the pumper. A hose sprayed water from the tanker wagon onto the blacksmith shop and stacks of hay at the stables.

I fell over a heavy, yielding mass in the middle of the road. By the flickering light, I saw the body of a dead, scorched horse, still warm to the touch.

Mrs. Steckler stood by a bucket brigade going from the pump on the corner to the Palmer House. She was yelling, "Do something. Do something." I looked for Annie. She could be anywhere in this press of people.

But she wasn't. In the garish light, I saw the curtains move in the window of my old room. Next to these there was something whiter than the curtains. I remembered Annie's shackles. She was trying to free herself from the bedstead. I was frantic for her. Flames had jumped to the tree that overhung the Palmer House woodshed, and flaming branches dropped onto the metal roof.

Someone tugged at my hair. I looked up at Mr. Collins, sitting on horseback right in back of me.

"Give me your hand, Maude, and swing up behind me," he yelled.

"No. Annie's trapped in the Palmer House. She can't get loose."

"Come on," he yelled. "I've got to get my horses out of the corral."

"No," I yelled. "You come help me. I'm going to go get Annie out of Palmer House."

"Annie? You mean that Indian?" His horse danced sideways away from the heat.

"Yes. Won't you help me?"

"I've got to get my horses." He spurred his horse into the darkness.

There was no time to waste. I flew to the back steps and up them. The heat was so strong as to seem to push me. The door at the top of the stairs was unbolted. However, the door to my room was firmly fastened. I threw my shoulder against it and yelled at Annie to open it. She did, and hot air rushed past me. She had torn the bed apart and was standing just inside the door holding the end of the metal bedstead in her hands.

I took my knife from my pocket and sliced the leather manacle to free her. I grabbed Annie's arm, but she wrenched away and began to scrabble at the floor. After lifting a piece of board, she pulled a metal cigar box from under the floor.

Again I grabbed her, but as soon as I stuck my head out the door I saw the stairs were in flames. Holding tight to Annie, I crossed the room and threw up the window. Immediately, I knew I should have closed the room door because the heat surged around us. The metal roof shrieked as it heated up. I yelled and screamed and waved the white curtains. Almost immediately, two firemen ran with a short wooden ladder.

They had barely got the bottom end secured when I was out the window and hanging until my feet touched the top rung. I went down two rungs until I could steady myself.

Then I yelled and tugged at Annie until she came out the window feet first. I don't know where I got the strength, Mama, but I held her and eased her down between me and the wall until her feet were on the top rung. She clung to that box with one hand so that she was using only the other to grasp the ladder.

One of the firemen started up the ladder to help, but the ladder bent under the added weight, so he waited until we reached the bottom.

Annie was shivering, and her eyes rolled about like those of a panicked horse. One of the firemen put a blanket around her. Another put a coat around me. They led us away from the danger and left us in front of the schoolhouse.

My knees just gave way, and I pulled Annie down with me on the steps. The whole Main Street of Eldorado was on fire. The very window of the Palmer House from which we had just escaped looked like the mouth of Daniel's burning fiery furnace. The roof fell in clattering sections. The Centennial Bar was aflame. Next to it, the adobe walls of the Mercantile held, but flames flickered from the roof. In all the orange light, you could see as plain as day.

Three horsemen came down the street herding a bunch of horses. One of the horsemen clattered to a stop. Cody Collins dismounted and stood in front of us. "Are you all right, Maude?" he yelled, even though there was no need over here away from the frenzy.

I shook my head yes.

"Is this Annie? Is she all right?"

"Yes. She's scraped and scared some. She's still trembling."

"Up at the fire, someone said you went upstairs all alone and saved the Indian."

"Well, I couldn't have got out of there if it hadn't been for the firemen. They helped us get out the window.

163

Doubtless one of them would have gone after Annie if they'd known she was there."

"Well, if that don't beat all," he said. "Now that took true grit." There was such admiration in his voice that I felt like I had done a man's job.

After a moment, he asked, "How come the Indian couldn't come down those steps by herself? Is she crippled or something?"

I told him about Mrs. Steckler chaining Annie to the bed. Then I told him about Mrs. Steckler throwing me out and where I was staying. It didn't make one lick of difference to him. He just said, "That old cow."

He continued, "You've sure got what it takes to be a ranch wife. Have you made up your mind yet?"

I must have looked pitiful at him because he said with a funny laugh, "There's not much to hold you here. The town's almost all burned down, the biggest mining company closed its office, and the stamping mill shut down this very night."

"About all I've got left is my debt at the Mercantile. How I'm ever going to pay it without a job, I don't know."

"You don't have to pay for a dead horse, you know," he said. He sat beside me but on a lower step. I was still holding Annie.

"Yes, it's owed, and I'll pay it. Continental owned the store, so when I can I'll pay the debt to the Continental Mine office in Denver."

He shifted around some and cleared his throat a couple of times. "Don't be sending them any money, Miss Maude. Your debt was taken care of," he said.

"Whatever do you mean?"

He dropped his head so I couldn't see his face.

"You did it, didn't you?" I asked.

I shifted Annie to the side and bent down to lift his hat from his head. While he looked at me surprised, I kissed him on the cheek. "Cody Collins," I said, "you're four-square. I thank you. But I'll repay you for that debt, just like I'll do for any debt I owe."

I took a deep breath and added, "I can't give you an answer yet. My mind's all a muddle from everything happening all at once."

But, Mama, sitting here now, writing and waiting for Annie to awaken, I know the answer I'm going to give him. I have to tell him no. Mr. Collins would make a fine, kind husband. But I don't want to be a ranch wife. And I don't love him. When I marry a man I want to experience the love Mr. Shakespeare wrote about.

I see now that I do have true grit. I don't have a cent to my name. But I have strength of body and spirit, enough to carry me on any path I choose to go. And I must have something like Da's gold fever. But my gold fever is some power that drives me to carve or draw, and I'm not going to say no to that power. I'm going to aim at being an artist. It might take a while since I'll have to work to support myself while I study. There's Annie, too. While she's a hard worker, she needs someone to look after her, at least for now.

I guess you could say, Mama, that I want everything. I want to be an artist. I want to love a man and marry him. I want to take care of Annie until she doesn't need me anymore. I want the moon and stars. All of them, even the stars in mighty Orion.

Thursday, March 4, 1897

Mama, I never cease to be amazed at how things turn out. After losing my job, spending two nights in a bawdyhouse, and turning down an offer of marriage from a prosperous man, I was at my wit's end about what to do next. I couldn't stay in Eldorado, but I couldn't afford to leave.

Yet, here I sit today in the Santa Cecilia train station in new clothes with two tickets for Santa Fe in my purse. And Annie and I had a restful night, having spent it as guests in a room at the boardinghouse here. We sat at the dining-room table and were waited on like regular ladies. There was some hesitation at letting an Indian sit at table with white people, but I just looked the landlady in the eye and said, "She's my sister."

Like a shy child Annie stays close by my side. Though she whispers to me, she's not spoken to anyone else yet. Despite being a little scared to be out in the world, she's happy, too. She keeps smoothing out her new calico dress and adjusting her new shawl. Then her hand creeps up to her ears to be sure her new gold earrings are still there. I'm wearing one of Big Effie's skirts, mine having got pretty well scorched in the fire.

My shawl is the one Lovey gave me. But I have a new shirtwaist and a new purse. There's not many ready-made clothes in the store here that will fit me.

As to how this amazing change came about, I owe it all to Annie. Yesterday, as we were taking stock of our situation and I was trying to figure out what to do, Annie bolted the door to our room at Miss Peggy's. She pulled up her skirt and brought out the battered tin tobacco box, the very one she saved from the fire. She had tied it into a sling which was wrapped around her waist. Then I heard the first words from her mouth since that awful night Flem beat her up. "Take this," she said. The box was heavy. When I took the lid off I thought I saw sand. Then I realized Annie had a box of gold dust. I was struck speechless.

When I had somewhat recovered, Annie told me in words and signs how she came to have it. During those years when she cleaned out the Centennial Bar, she had turned the filthy, smelly sawdust into her own gold mine. Many miners paid for their whiskey and gambling debts with gold. At the end of the bar, there was kept a little scale for weighing it out. Due to carelessness, no doubt caused by strong drink, much dust fell to the floor. Annie gathered the sawdust from under the bar and took it in a gunny sack to the woodshed in back of the Palmer House. She shut herself inside and with a pipe stem blew the sawdust away from the heavier gold.

Now, Mama, wasn't she a smart girl to do that? But she was even smarter. She knew if anyone else knew about the gold, they'd take it. She even thought Flem came to her room to take her gold. Also, she knows that if she tries to trade it for money or anything else, she'll be cheated because she's an Indian.

"I can't take your gold," I said to Annie.

"Sisters?" she said.

"Yes, we can be sisters, but I can't take your money. I'll help you so no one can cheat you."

"We're sisters. We help one another." She refused to take the box back. There's no point arguing with one stubborn enough to keep silent for years.

So we're traveling to Santa Fe on her money. But I'll be very sparing of the use of it and try to preserve it for her until she's educated enough to make decisions.

We'll both work in Santa Fe. Mr. Jennings says there are hotels and restaurants there. There are also Indians in that area. Maybe Annie can get acquainted with them and learn how to be an Indian if that's what she wants.

As for me, I'm so happy, I'm like to bust. Mr. Jennings is going to start me in his sketching class. He is right here at this very station to go to Santa Fe also. Miss Katy is here in her pretty green riding habit to see him off.

She came over to the bench where Annie and I were sitting and said, "I have something to say to you privately." She looked at Annie.

I said, "It's all right, Miss Katy, she's my sister."

Miss Katy gave me a little packet wrapped in a bit of soft cotton cloth. "Cody sent this to you. It was our grandmother's. He wants you to have it as a remembrance." Inside the cloth was a silver filigree brooch set with a garnet. This token of esteem from that tough cowboy made me weep a little.

While I blew my nose and averted my eyes, there was a clatter of excitement as a buggy drew up at the station. It was Miss Peggy's. I'd been watching for it as my trunk was to come down on it. Venus alighted from the buggy. Every male eye in the place was on her. She looked the perfect lady in her navy blue suit and little hat with the veil over one eye. She directed the unloading of much baggage, then looked around.

As soon as she saw me she started toward me. I was quite surprised to see her here because when Annie and I left the house yesterday to walk to Santa Cecilia, she was awaiting the arrival of her generous gentleman friend.

"There you are," she said gaily.

Miss Katy looked curious and expectant, so I began introductions. "Miss Katherine Gynne, may I introduce my friend . . ."

Venus interrupted me. "Yes. I'm Maude's friend, Elizabeth Oakley St. John. So happy to meet you, Miss Gynne."

Venus smiled quite warmly at the three of us. She might have just come from an afternoon tea instead of Peacock Gulch. "Such a flurry to get packed at such short notice. But we just received word that an old family friend we had been expecting had to cancel his visit. So why wait? I thought. I'll just hurry and catch the same train as Maude so we can travel as far as Albuquerque together."

"Is Albuquerque your final destination, then?" Miss Katy asked.

"Oh, no. I'm going back East to school. Daddy says

I'm turning into a regular savage living on the ranch. He wants me to have the advantage of an Eastern education," Venus said.

Miss Katy looked puzzled. "I don't believe I know any rancher in these parts by the name of St. John."

"Oh, look," Venus said, pointing discreetly with her gloved finger. "I think that gentleman over there is trying to get your attention." Miss Katy said her farewells to us and hurried to join Mr. Jennings.

My mouth still stood open in astonishment. "Elizabeth Oakley St. John?" I asked.

"Don't you like it? I thought your middle name sounded just right."

"Venus, you do take the cake," I said.

"I hope so. I'd better go get my ticket."

"Wait," I said. "I want to show you something." I showed her the brooch. "What do you think? Does Cody Collins really love me?" I asked Venus.

"Probably. But he'll get over it. As the Great Bard said, 'Men have died from time to time, and worms have eaten them, but not for love.' " She swept away to the ticket counter.

Mama, I must end now. I don't feel your spirit as constantly with me as I once did. I think I know why. In these past few days, I've shown you, and myself, that I've gained enough judgment and strength to overcome the adversities of life.

Bless you, Mama. I'll now let you rest in peace with the angels. I'm going to leave off writing about my troubles and begin living my life.